FEMINA REAL

This collection of nine short stories contains some of A. L. Barker's most powerful and disquieting writing to date. *Noon*, set in a seaside holiday hotel, memorably expresses the ambivalence and repression in the lives of ordinary, respectable people in a story about a middle-aged man's unacknowledged trysts with a young girl. In *Glory, Glory Allelujah* an ageing brother and sister attempt to exorcise the imprisoned hopelessness of their lives, imposed by their dead monster of a mother, in a ritual bonfire.

FEMINA REAL

By

A. L. BARKER

1971
THE HOGARTH PRESS
LONDON

Published by
The Hogarth Press Ltd
40–42 William IV Street
London WC2

★

Clarke, Irwin and Co Ltd
Toronto

ISBN 0 7012 0352 8

Printed in Great Britain by
Ebenezer Baylis & Son Limited
The Trinity Press, Worcester and London

To Dorothy

ACKNOWLEDGEMENTS

The author makes acknowledgements to the editors of *Nova* in which the story *Noon* first appeared, and to Penguin Books Ltd. who first published *Almost an International Incident* in *Penguin Modern Stories 8* (1971) and to the Arts Council of Great Britain, with whose financial encouragement this book was written.

CONTENTS

La Matière

PERHAPS Marty had never actually heard her mother say, 'This child is a challenge'. But it could justifiably have been said—there had always been so much mettle between them. Uttered or not, the words went into Marty's secret history and she didn't question them although she pondered whether she would have seemed a challenge to another parent. But when she observed other parents she concluded that it had been her own doing, in the womb, before she was conscious of doing anything, and if another mother could not see the challenge that would be because she could not meet it.

Which was hardly surprising. A challenge of Marty's magnitude took some meeting. It took singlemindedness, selflessness, ruthlessness, negative and positive virtues, and every trick in the book. Like the one which was also part of Marty's secret history.

How did she know so much about the business behind her first school? Did she surmise that utterly selfless manœuvre, regardless of her own happiness, by which her mother had done her best for her daughter? Marty could only have been seven or eight years old, how had she come by her knowledge? It was really adult secret history first and foremost and only incidentally Marty's.

Troy House had been a nightmare, four nightmare years. It was the best school in the district, pupils had to be bright as well as rich. Marty was just able to put two and two together.

'She's a late developer. She'll go the farther and she needs teachers of the finest.'

Marty's mother was Nadia Belletout, the daughter of a

French lawyer. She had been educated in a convent where the star pupil was the one who made the best lobster bisque, the Mother Superior's favourite dish. Nadia believed in education and in Marty because Marty was her daughter. 'Au fond,' she said, 'is la matière.'

They both believed in this substance, indeed Marty lived in hope. As a child she longed for it. She watched and waited, she thought it must be there because her mother had said so: her mother, she was given to understand, had put it there. She dreamed of it surfacing and astounding them all. She thought at first of being famous, her name on everyone's lips, in books, in newspapers, on foundation stones, her name and her mother's. She saw her mother proud and satisfied, she did want her mother to be satisfied. Later, she thought that substance was a name for quality and that she would turn out to be of very rare quality. She would be unique among people. Later still she worried that the substance might be too far down ever to come to the top. Finally, it was borne in upon her that there was no substance.

As a child of eight she wasn't yet aware of la matière. She knew that something was expected of her and not knowing what it was, felt guilty. Peter Prout, her father, said that she made him believe in the doctrine of original sin.

Troy House was presided over by a Dr. Highsmith. Two surprising facts emerged when Marty pointed out that she wasn't ill and didn't want to go to a doctor: Dr. Highsmith had nothing to do with medicine and she was a woman.

'She wants to talk to you,' said Marty's mother, 'to see what sort of little girl you are.'

Marty immediately began to worry. Suppose she was already the wrong sort? This doctor would find it out.

'I want you to talk to her intelligently, answer her questions, tell her what she wants to know. You are not to stutter or hold your breath or push out your lip as you are doing now. You are to consider before you speak, but not too long. And be careful, she will try to trap you. Don't think that because you are a child she will have pity.'

'You'll frighten her out of her wits,' said Marty's father.

'Il ne faut pas qu'elle fasse une betise.'

Apparently Dr. Highsmith insisted on a preliminary interview which was in the nature of an examination. Intending pupils had to know a certain amount before she would undertake to teach them more and so Marty was crammed with general knowledge. Besides the twelve times table and the capital of India and the banners of the Union Jack and the personal pronouns she had to recite the rivers and counties of England.

On the day of the interview she was sick with dread. She had not slept for fighting all night long to hold on to her knowledge. First one fact then another had simply slipped away, walking between her parents up the steps of Troy House she did not know her own name.

Dr. Highsmith turned out to be young and very pretty and this further confounded Marty's confusion. It was such diabolical cleverness to have a full white bosom gently lifting under the black lace of her dress while she asked demolishing questions.

'Who is your favourite author? How many metals did you see on your way here? What colour is the door of this house?'

'She takes after me, she is not observant,' said Marty's mother. 'We live a great deal in our thoughts.'

'I think it will be best if you leave us so that your daughter and I can talk alone together.' Dr. Highsmith struck a silver bell on her desk. 'My secretary will take you to see the song and dance class.'

'Don't expect a flow,' said Marty's father. 'You know what they say about still waters?'

Dr. Highsmith smiled. 'I know.'

When they were alone she propped her fine white elbows on the desk and rested her chin on her hands and looked at Marty. Marty's hands were sweating on the palms. It was the end of the world, why did it have to come like this, through a bright, sharp, tin goddess? Full of the bitterness of defeat, she clenched her fists.

'What's the matter, Marty?'

Marty could have told her! But she didn't speak one word, though the lady kept her voice sweet and low and tried to interest her in a tiny geographical globe which she had on her desk. Marty shook her head or nodded when directly appealed to and would not look up from her thumbs.

Presently the secretary came back to see if the interview was over. Dr. Highsmith's voice was still sweet and low but Marty heard her say, 'I'm afraid the child is a lummox.'

To Mr. and Mrs. Prout she kept her voice sweet but not so low.

'You see, I am not a crusader. I give my best as a teacher but I can give only to the best pupils.'

'Marty will be an excellent pupil.'

'Indeed, but not if we force the pace.'

'Are you saying that she is slow?'

'I am saying that her mind does not move in the same way as other children's. It does not mean that she will be left behind, she may arrive as soon, or sooner—'

'The tortoise and the hare?' suggested Marty's father.

'—but she would be at a disadvantage here,' said Dr. Highsmith as if he had not spoken.

'I will be the judge of that.'

'I beg your pardon, Mrs. Prout, but can you? Without knowing intimately our curriculum, our achievements, our ambitions, and the potential of each child at Troy House?'

Nadia put her finger under Marty's chin and lifted it. To Marty the sensation was a painful one, bringing her back into a hateful situation and reminding her that she was the crux of it.

'Where I come from we do things differently. It is those who pay who have the choice.'

Dr. Highsmith revealed slightly fluted teeth when she smiled. 'But presumably those who sell may first choose the price?'

Nadia sat back in her chair, drawing Marty to her with a warm gesture of pride. It chilled Marty to the bone, for what had she to be proud about?

'You would find us very comprehending. If the school needed to raise funds, anything like that, we should wish to be associated, we should have your good causes at heart. Naturellement.'

Dr. Highsmith leaned forward and snapped her fingers under Marty's nose. 'What is the Holy Trinity?'

'He, she, it,' said Marty.

How frequently was her name spoken between her father and Dr. Highsmith? It began with his saying, as they came away from Troy House, 'Well, that's that,' and Nadia saying, 'It is not that, it is this: I am going to get Marty into that school.'

'My dear, there are plenty of other schoolmarms who'd be glad to take her.'

'That one takes the children of our friends, why does she refuse my daughter?'

Marty's father sharpened the point of his beard with his finger-tips. 'She shows an independent spirit, certainly.'

'Is it nothing to you that I shall be ridiculous? People will say we have a booby, une petite ballourde. You must speak again to this professeur.'

'I?'

'Who else? You are the child's father, if she has short measure it is you who gave it.'

So Peter Prout spoke to Dr. Highsmith. What did he say? Marty had no idea, it was all Olympian to her. When he returned, smiling, from the encounter, she realised for the first time that enemies did not necessarily carry daggers.

'Verdict suspended,' he said gaily. 'Marty may be presumed

intelligent until proved otherwise. She will get another trial, a
written one.'

'Is it our money which is not fit to be paid?' cried Nadia.
'Shall not this woman be tried also?'

'That's a clever little lady,' said Peter Prout. 'She has ideals
and makes other people pay for them.'

He took Marty back to Troy House and Dr. Highsmith sat
her at her own desk with sheets of ruled paper and two new
pencils, very sharp, and a pure white rubber.

'You have half an hour, Marty, to answer six questions — five
minutes for each. Here they are, they are not difficult. It is now
half-past three, we'll come back at four and see how you have
got on.'

'Good luck, pigeon,' said Peter Prout and winked as he went
out.

Marty wondered why he had called her that. He had never
done so before, he did not use such terms and she was not in
the least like a pigeon. It was all wrong, for her and for him,
awfully wrong, the awfulness she felt but did not understand.

Moments passed before she picked up the list of questions.
They were incomprehensible. She had forgotten how to read,
she could not even identify the marks on the paper. What was
the matter with her? What was she? Was she something they
were going to find out about? Was she a false pretence? If so,
whose — since all she wanted was to be real?

The miniature geographical globe on Dr. Highsmith's
desk — when Marty set it spinning the greens and browns and
blues rolled into one. People said, if she had understood them
aright, that this was how the world went, round and round, with
no colour and no pattern. That seemed like another pretence.

She returned to the questions. The first two were sums.
They took her a long time to do because she had to work
them out on her fingers — even the multiplication one because
she had forgotten her tables — and then she broke one of the
new pencils. The beautiful point snapped with a noise like a

gun-shot. She looked for somewhere to hide, somewhere to get forgotten because now she was not only hopeless she was damned and if there were deeper depths she was for them.

'What is a circle?'

She couldn't answer that, not if she had twenty new pencils.

There was a foot-muff of soft white fur under Dr. Highsmith's desk. Marty knelt on the floor and her skin crept away from the fur. She had had a pet rabbit, a beautiful red-eyed doe, which ate its young as soon as it had given them birth. Marty's mother made her watch the whole thing. She said, 'There can be no secrets until you are a woman.'

There was, however, the secret which Marty had managed to keep, even while the white rabbit swallowed its own flesh and blood. But how much longer could she keep it from Dr. Highsmith who did not look at Marty's tongue or take her temperature because she could read her like a book?

What was a lummox?

Nowadays Marty couldn't bear rabbits. She had nightmares about fur, soft white fur turned her stomach.

Peter Prout and the Doctor didn't see her under the desk. They came back at four o'clock and he said, 'She's finished the paper and gone off somewhere.'

'She should have waited. Children shouldn't dismiss themselves.'

'Marty's a wanderer. You'll have to teach her to stand still for the National Anthem. Let's see what she's written.'

'Give me the paper, please.'

'Shall I read you the answers?' His foot lightly struck the other side of the panel as he bent over the desk. 'Questions one and two are sums, addition and multiplication and she's done them both. Oh excellent! What powers of deduction! Question three: "What is a circle?" Answer: "A ring with a hole in it." Could you do better than that?'

He was laughing but Dr. Highsmith said sharply, 'I'd like to see the paper.'

'Don't you trust me?'

'No.'

'It would be unflattering if you did. Question four: "What is the capital of London?" Ah, is that fair? It's two jumps ahead of the poor little devil. She's too young to think her elders and betters could be wrong, let alone suspect them of being wrong on purpose.' The desk creaked as he perched himself on the edge.

Dr. Highsmith came and stood beside Marty at the knee-hole. 'They were very simple sums but she hasn't got them right.'

'It shows she needs to go to school.'

'She hasn't even attempted the general intelligence questions.'

'You'll take her, won't you?'

'I'm sorry.'

'For my sake?'

'Why yours?'

His voice was soft and Dr. Highsmith's had lost its edge. They were not talking about Marty now. She had noticed that people's voices changed when they stopped talking about her, or to her. She noticed this in her mother's most of all.

'For one thing, Nadia will make my life hell if you don't. For another, it'll give me an excuse for coming here.'

'I cannot abandon my principles.'

'A woman as pretty as you has principles only to abandon them.'

'Your marital relations are no concern of mine.' Dr. Highsmith crossed her ankles and Marty shrank back to avoid being kicked in the face. 'And why should you want to come here again?'

Marty had put her hand into soft white fur and was sick over Dr. Highsmith's foot-muff.

*　　*　　*

It was a battle among gods, but Dr. Highsmith was no match for Nadia Prout who nodded when her husband told her that Marty had failed the test.

'You must speak to the teacher again.'

'My dear, she has principles. What can you do with a woman like that?'

Nadia smiled. 'I leave it to you.'

Peter Prout wasn't such a god himself. He came somewhere between Marty and Olympus. He asked Marty more in exasperation than hope, 'What does she expect? You're made of the same stuff, you must know.'

He stood sharpening his beard with his finger-tips and looking Marty's way. If he had ever actually looked at her he might have wondered about the stuff and it would have helped to know that someone else was ready, or at any rate willing, to see a difference.

Marty understood that she would be going to Troy House, nothing could stop it. To her friends, Nadia Prout said, 'We think of sending Marty to Troy House. I suppose one can do no better?'

What Peter Prout was thinking had little to do with Marty. If he recognised her connection he was non-committal. He became quite Gallic with his shrugs and gestures. But it seemed that he spoke again to Dr. Highsmith. Again and again.

'What made you think it would do any good? Or that I would have time? You know that more and more of my leisure is sacrificed to business. It's no use I tell you, she's adamant. I'll have no part in such nonsense.'

And then his sleep had to be sacrificed to business, some nights he did not come home at all.

'You've no conception,' he told Nadia, 'what it takes in goodwill and hospitality to secure one contract.'

'Could I help with the hospitality?'

'They aren't the sort of people I'd care to bring here.'

'But it's so expensive entertaining in hotels?'

'It does put up the costs rather — to them.'

Marty went on working with a governess in the mornings and playing in the Gardens in the afternoons. Those were the days when walking a clean wooden hoop along a path was called 'playing'. To Marty it was more like the labour of Sisyphus, she had such a job keeping her hoop upright and preventing it from running between gentlemen's legs. When her mother met friends in the Gardens Marty was required to keep company with the friends' children, most of whom went to Troy Park. They did not roll hoops. The girls did complicated steps with skipping-ropes and the boys asked her riddles or drove her hoop into the fishpond. They had heard their mothers say what irony that someone as beautiful and clever as Nadia should have a plain, dull daughter. Peter Prout, too, was handsome and spirited, it went to show how superficial their attributes must be, not even skin deep.

How long did it take? In those days Marty only knew time as a beginning and an ending and feared them both. Managing as desperately as she did, anything new was a threat. Every day her mother tried to prepare her.

'Put your shoulders back and hold up your head. Do not make your feet like spoons. Place them so, the heel of one before the toe of the other. Smile when people speak to you. But without showing your teeth, please, when you have a gap in front.'

Was she preparing Marty for Troy House? Or for life? Not for Dr. Highsmith, anyway, *she* no longer required special consideration.

'What are twelve pennies? Five times five? Where is the Eiffel Tower?'

Perhaps she was looking for 'la matière'. As for Marty, she simply went on trying and hoping, she was like a little dog jumping again and again with bursting heart at a stick held out of reach.

It came too soon. Marty understood nothing, but by some kind of osmosis or the feeling in the air she knew that Troy

House would now start. She was in her mother's room that evening when her father came to say that he would not be home to dinner.

'We are going out, you and I,' said Nadia. 'To the Courtaulds' and after to the theatre.'

'Damn! I'd forgotten.'

'How could you? It was for you it was arranged, to see the Coward's play.'

'The Coward play,' said Peter. 'Well, it's impossible. You'll have to make my apologies. I'll be in Bradford with provincial buyers all the evening.'

'And all the night?'

'Not worth travelling two hundred miles to go to bed here, is it?'

'That would depend who you go to bed with.' Nadia tapped Marty's mouth. 'Ferme ta bouche, you are not to have a lip like a jug.' She smiled at her husband. 'I am asking myself what can this professeur of little children teach you? You have no vocation so it cannot be that you are teaching her.'

'Teaching who?'

'You are too lazy. Besides, what do you know that everyone else does not?'

'I don't know what you're talking about!'

He was no actor and he was rather nervous of his wife. He began shouting before he had had time to be bewildered, or to pretend to be. It was a mistake, with Nadia it was an added disadvantage to be in the state where shouting was necessary. Marty could have told him that.

'Do you suppose I want to be working when I could be at the theatre? I don't *enjoy* making money but I accept my responsibilities.'

'Do you deny that you will be with Dr. Highsmith tonight?'

'Of course I deny it!'

'And that when you have not gone to bed here nor in Bradford you have gone to bed with her?'

'I deny it, I deny it!'

'And that you have a key to her door and a robe-de-chambre and slippers, and when the little children are gone you are alone with her—'

'No, no, no!' He pounded his fist on the table.

Marty bit her lips to keep them closed. Did he think noise would help him?

'And that she makes you a tisane before you go to bed with her? Why a tisane?' Nadia smiled. 'It does not seem appropriate.'

'It's a lie, every word's a thundering lie!'

'I must tell you that you have been watched.'

'Watched?'

'I paid someone to do it.'

'You mean a private detective?'

'They call themselves confidential agents. It was so very confidential.'

Peter Prout unclenched his hand and rubbed it across his chest as if it were sticky.

'You had me watched?' His usually pale face was brick red and Marty feared he was going to cry. 'My God,' he said thickly and turned his back on them both.

'I have plenty of evidence. Naturellement, it is what I paid for.'

'What do you want?'

'We will speak of what I want. And then you will speak to Dr. Highsmith of what she does not want. I do not need to remind you that as a teacher of young children there are things she cannot want?'

'For God's sake—'

'You know very well whose sake it is for.' Nadia took Marty by the shoulders and pushed her away. 'Go and plait your hair, child, it is so dreadfully straight.'

*　　*　　*

'Unfortunate' was a word spoken of Marty by the time she was seventeen. It seemed to many people that she so easily need not have been what she was. A little more or a little less and she might have been passably pretty or plain: the Prouts had so much money that 'passably' was the operative word.

There was something about her which, while not exactly stopping, was definitely hindering. 'Like those women in Dutch interiors', someone said, 'with true beauty and faces like pudding'.

'A little more blood and a little less nose would be an improvement.'

Nadia was wont to remark, in a humbling tone, 'On my side she is related to the Orloffs', and since her friends usually did what she expected of them they were humbled. Even if they rebelled when she was out of earshot.

'Who are the Orloffs, anyway?'

'Petty dynasts.'

'For a nose like that one should have only the Tsar to thank.'

Marty could look beautiful in repose but she rarely reposed in public. She had an expression, almost another face, compounded from a lifetime of doubt. It was in her eyes, the way she held her head sideways as if to listen, slanting that nose of hers so that it caught unnecessary light along its pale length. That was how people mostly saw her and were hindered, even the hardiest of them, by the thought that there was something they should be saying. But what?

Marty wasn't waiting for their help, she didn't know that she looked as if she was, had long since ceased to think that anyone could do anything for her.

Her longing and dreaming, even her adolescent dreaming, revolved and relied on getting an answer to her question. When she prayed to God the Mother she prayed for knowledge for there could be no greater mercy than knowing what was expected of her.

Nadia, of course, always made her designs known. She

designed the Wyldecks' picnic, for instance, as Marty's entrée into the Wyldeck family. While they were thinking of a simple frivol on a summer's day Nadia was founding a dynasty.

'It will be an excellent thing. I have discussed it with George and Minnie Wyldeck and we are agreed.'

A marriage was being arranged, Marty was being parcelled up exclusively and permanently with another human being. But since she wasn't a parcel, not quite, and there was another human being involved, an encounter had first to be arranged.

'Hugo Wyldeck will have a hundred thousand pounds. Also,' said Nadia, 'the Wyldeck Steel Corporation.'

'Suppose he doesn't like me?' said Marty.

'It's up to you to make him.'

As if she didn't know, hadn't already seen this new stick to jump for. Was it higher than ever? Or a little lower than usual? That would depend on Hugo Wyldeck's expectations. How did you make a young man like you enough to want to marry you? Marty had no idea, she had never had time to think about it.

'Why push it?' said Peter Prout. He sometimes had twinges about Marty, nothing serious because she was, after all, her mother's daughter. 'There are plenty of other young men.'

'Whose name is not Wyldeck.'

Marty crept away to look at herself in a mirror. It did no more than confirm that she had the regulation two eyes, nose and mouth and that her hair would not curl. It was not the first time she had looked and despaired, but now she was looking for something different, with less chance of finding it.

She remembered the girls at school saying, 'You must look as if you're ready to, even if you're not.'

How had they looked, those girls? Pretty, of course, they had all been pretty. But Marty was ready to—if it would help. She put her head on her arms and wept.

The Wyldecks' picnic was in the nature of a field banquet at their country estate at Belfont, a place that neither grew nor grazed towards its upkeep. Wooden gazebos were erected beside the river, and blue and gold tents, the trees were wired for lights and music. Animals were roasted whole over spits and ice boxes were brought for the champagne. Old Lord Wyldeck, nearly dead but still a peer, was floated to the picnic in a flat-bottomed boat and given sips of blood-heat Chateau d'Yquem from a thermos.

Everything was organised, including the weather. The weather did not venture to incommode the Wyldecks, it brought out a tawny day from much farther south, Italy or Spain.

'Perfect for a picnic,' said Nadia, as she helped Marty to dress. 'You mustn't wear voile, it is not distinguée. Put on this wild silk and a bandeau à la Turcq.'

'It always comes untied—'

'Not the way I tie it. Remember, you are to engage this young man—'

'Oh not today! Mother, I can't possibly make him propose today!'

'You are to engage his attentions,' said Nadia firmly. 'That is how to start.'

It seemed to Marty that all her life she had been starting and never finishing. Had she found a way of getting through on potential, receiving the benefit, always, of the doubt? Could one, she wondered wildly, engage and capture a young man's fancy by being ready to start?

She knew hardly anyone at the picnic. Out of delicacy Nadia had declined the invitation for herself and Peter because she believed that Marty should handle this piece of personal engineering entirely on her own.

It was an act of confidence which filled Marty with the old familiar anguish. Once again she was going forth under sickeningly high hopes. Could she continue to fall so far below them without reaching rock bottom? Couldn't she get to a point of some return? Couldn't she start to feel a little less bad about her failures?

Hugo Wyldeck had softly waving hair the colour of wheat and all his shaving could not make stubble of the peach-like down on his cheeks. Marty remembered not to twitch her upper lip when they were introduced.

'So you're Marty Prout,' he said and walked round her with his hands in his pockets, quite frankly looking her over. She feared he would ask his mother to lead her up and down as if she were a horse.

'I suppose you can dance?'

He escorted her through the crowd to the dance floor erected under the limes and Marty, with her hand held cere-moniously high in his, hoped that she didn't look as silly as she felt. Hugo Wyldeck's stately manner was more suited to powdered wigs and minuets than cricket shirts and fox-trotting.

'I was told you're a charming girl.'

Marty smiled desperately, recognising the stick. At least she danced nicely, she hoped he noticed. On the waxed boards under the limes they went well together. Of course it wouldn't be enough but it might favourably dispose him.

'I'm told you're kind,' he said.

'Oh, I think I am.'

'You don't seem sure.'

'Well I try to be kind.'

'That's no use, people who try to be kind are usually mon-sters.'

How should she engage his attentions? Ought she to say that she had piloted Blue Bird, knew Aly Khan, marched in protest, hunger-struck?

'You don't look English.' He was very suspicious.

'Oh I am.'

'I was told you're half Russian.'

'Not half, not even a quarter.' Was she wrong in assuming

the idea didn't appeal to him? But it had ever so slightly engaged his attention. 'My great-grandmother was an Orloff, I suppose that makes me one-eighth Russian.'

The band played 'If You Were the Only Girl in the World', it was an injunction to them both. Marty felt everyone giving them knowing looks, she was used to being common knowledge, her mother's eye being better than God's in that it looked at her out of everyone.

'Nauseating,' said Hugo.

'What is?'

'The mater's taste in music. In anything.' Marty did not miss the coldness of his tone nor the fact that his hand merely pegged hers up as they danced. 'I'll cut loose as soon as I come of age and set up on my own. You won't see me at Belfont.'

Would she see him anywhere else? The girls at school, melting or butterfly girls, how they had succeeded, even the least of them! They had managed to make a risk out of the same old place and time, out of some secret words they made a challenge which no young man could ignore. Marty was no butterfly: could she melt — with that nose?

'I don't care for the imitative copulative act,' said Hugo.

'I beg your pardon?'

'Dancing, I don't like it.'

That was a pity, but 'Neither do I,' said Marty quickly.

'Then let's not.'

They left the dance floor and walked under the trees. It was being an excellent picnic, the bunting greener and redder and gayer than ordinary, the sunlight deep and even and not at all crisp, and aprons of shade under every tree for those who wanted it. And there was the band to sweeten thought and as far as the lifted eye could see was Wyldeck country, trimmed and tidy and ready to paint.

'How pretty it is,' Marty said wistfully. 'Everyone must be very happy.'

'I'll tell you what, this place is a great big dead donkey.

It's been hung round my grandfather's neck and it'll hang round my father's but I'm damned if it'll hang round mine.'

'What will you do?'

'Sell it, lock and barrel. There's no stock, nor much barrel either.'

'But where will you live?'

'In Sunderland, where the plant is.'

'Plant?'

'Wyldeck Steel,' he said impatiently, and in the same breath, 'I'll get you an ice.' He shot away towards the refreshment tent, leaving her to follow.

Perhaps it was the group of girls who drew him. They broke and hovered and settled round him, they twittered and fluted his name and one clasped her two hands on his shoulder and hung on him as if she were all bright feathers and jewelled eyes.

That was certainly engaging, and ruthlessly done! Hugo hadn't a chance and he probably wouldn't have given Marty another thought. Why should he? He was engaged like a mid-sea island by a flock of swallows.

Marty had no hope but plenty of desperation. Not coming up to the mark was one thing, being dropped was another, she couldn't allow her mother's daughter to be dropped.

So she followed Hugo, stood at his occupied shoulder and told him yes, she would like an ice, a chocolate one.

'And what a good idea,' she said, 'to set up a telescope in the gazebo. Your mother can watch us from all that way off.'

Hugo muttered something and the girls trilled with laughter. The girl on his shoulder was like a humming-bird, clinging, trembling, vibrating with laughter. But he broke away and Marty was left confronting the aviary.

She wondered what other powers they had beside the power to engage. She was sure they were blessed with everything she lacked. And if there was so much, so randomly bestowed, didn't that make it almost standard, and what else could she be but sub-standard?

'You're Marty Prout.'

'The future Lady Wyldeck.'

'It's all arranged.'

'Imagine having your mother choose your husband!'

It ought to be possible, now that she had seen what these girls did, the gestures they made and the cries they uttered, it ought to be possible for her to do the same. She could put her heart into it, oh all her heart!

'I think it's feudal.'

'Mercenary.'

'Immoral.'

'Of course she isn't English. She's half French.'

'And half Russian.'

Marty was about to remind them that she had an English father when Hugo returned with the ice-cream in a long-stemmed glass. She might have enjoyed it, she had a young girl's appetite for sweet things, but not while the pretty birds watched her and Hugo frowned.

'Ice-cream is for babies.'

'It's fattening.'

The girl who had hung on Hugo's shoulder drew near to him again, but softly. 'I prefer a little Chablis — chilled, of course.'

Hugo said to Marty, 'I hope you're going to eat that. There are thousands of starving children who'd be glad to.'

A cry went up that the paper boat race was about to start. People turned towards the river, the young ones ran to where it brimmed lightning white out of the green grass. The river was suddenly tempting, full of possibilities, no one could think why they had stayed away from it. Whistles shrilled, and laughter, and the band struck up with 'Fly, bonnie boat'.

Of course the girls wanted to run and, abandoning his stateliness, so did Hugo. It was the moment to engage him with a gesture.

Marty tried, she flung out her arms and cried, 'Oh lovely,

27

lovely!' as the others were doing. She forgot that she had something in her hand.

The ball of ice-cream flew out of the glass and fell in a leaking chocolate arc. It dropped into the front of Hugo's open shirt. Marty would never forget the sound it made, the wet indecent plop! She blushed for it before she blushed for herself. Hugo's roar slowed even the rush to the river. People within hearing turned to look and others stopped and looked because they had an instinct for fuss.

'Oh dear!' cried Marty. 'Oh dear, oh dear!'

The girls of course laughed. They warbled and fluted and clucked and hooted with laughter.

Hugo's face was dark red, under his beautiful wheat gold hair his very scalp blazed. He reached inside his shirt and plucked out lumps of wet chocolate. It trickled down his fair white chest into the band of his trousers, a nauseous stain soaked through his silk shirt.

To Marty he said, 'You damned little Bolshie!' before he marched away across the meadow.

Marty stood in ruins. She could feel her mother watching: Nadia's eyebrows were up, delicately arched, her face entirely composed and disassociated from Marty's failure. In a moment she would lock it away in her heart with all the other failures and never refer to it again. And if anyone else did, she would wither the subject.

Marty turned and ran. She fell to pieces as she went – under trees, through hedges, across a gorsey place where brambles caught her, into ditches and over a gate marked 'Private, Trespassers will be summarily dealt with'. There was almost nothing left by the time she dropped to the ground in the depths of a wood.

She knelt with her hands over her face and her head on her knees. The grass under her cheek had more substance than she but she was used, by now, to finding la matière in everyone and everything else. She did wonder, often, what intent there was in making her so conspicuously without it. If there was intent to defraud, with herself as the instrument, how much longer could she bear it? Perhaps she had reached the limit, perhaps seventeen was the age to crack.

'If you're a Muslim, it's too early to pray.'

She looked up. A young man was twinkling at her through pebbled lenses.

'On the other hand, if you're a Muslim, you'd know that.'

'I wasn't praying.'

'At first I thought you were a clump of meadowsweet. Your dress is the same colour.'

It was a long time since anyone had thought her sweet. She sat up on her heels and the bandeau round her hair slid down on to her forehead. Probably no one had ever thought her like a flower.

'Meadowsweet?'

'It grows in damp places and smells nice. The flowers are yellowish-white cymes. What were you doing?'

'Nothing.'

'Actually it's a bit of a fraud.'

She scrambled to her feet. 'You've no right to say that. I wasn't trying to look like a flower.'

'I meant that the plant's a fraud. It doesn't produce any honey but insects are drawn to it by the scent and the florets are set so close together they're bound to get fertilised. I suppose it's one way to live.'

'I don't live that way.'

He lifted his glasses off his nose. 'I can see you don't,' and she believed him. Without the bright lenses his eyes were blunt, his face homely. Could one find home in a face?

'When I do nothing I do it like this.' He dropped to the grass, stretching himself on his back with his hands under his head. 'It shows I'm an ordinary chap. You now, you're extraordinary.'

'I'm sub-ordinary.' She smoothed her ruined dress over her knees. 'Can't you see that too?'

'No I can't.' He squinted up at her. 'And I should tell you that my eyesight's phenomenally good from this angle.'

The question was, what should she do now? If he hadn't come she wouldn't be asking, perhaps need never have asked, she might have stayed hidden in this wood, hunched on the ground and grown over with brambles—a Sleeping Ugliness.

'I ran away from the picnic and I'm afraid to go back. But I must.'

'Why must you?'

She shook her head, it was too long a story.

'A picnic's a shindig, either you enjoy it or you don't and you come away. There's no "must" about it, Miss Meadow-sweet. Do you mind if I call you that, minus the fraudulence?'

'My name's Marty Prout.'

He put on his glasses and pushed himself up on one elbow to look at her. 'So you're the girl they're going to marry my brother to.'

'Oh not any more! Not after what I did!'

'What did you do?'

She told him. 'He called me a Bolshie—because my great-grandmamma was an Orloff.'

'He's jealous. Poor old Hugo's a snob, he'd give anything to have a Russian grandmother. You're right, though, he'll never forgive you for throwing ice-cream at him.'

'Oh what can I do?'

'I should think you've done enough.'

'Don't laugh, it's serious—'

'Rubbish. You'd never get on with Hugo. I can't, and I've been trying for years. If Hugo's to make a good match he'll have to marry himself.'

It was strange that brothers should be so dissimilar. This young man had rough brown hair and a deeply freckled skin and huge bags at the knees of his grey flannel trousers.

'Hugo was named after a Wyldeck who fought at Agin-court and I was called Thomas, Richard, Henry because they had to baptise me in a hurry. Tom, Dick, Harry—you see? It didn't look as if I was going to need a name, they couldn't get me to yell when they held me up by the heels. I made up for it afterwards.'

Marty sometimes had a sensation as if an enormous load had been lifted and something that she had been afraid of all her life was never going to happen. But it only came when no one was looking at her. Tom Wyldeck might be so negligible that she could have this sensation in his presence, but suppose his presence had inspired it? She couldn't think of another reason why she should be having it now.

'Are you hungry?' said Tom.

'A little.'

'I've some chocolate.' He dug into his trousers pockets, bringing out a fishing-line and hooks, a padlock, a vaseline tin, a bunch of keys, a muddy handkerchief, a pipe full of dottle, a fan of spanners, some silver and an apple-core. 'Somewhere.' He threw the core away and delved again. 'Ah, here it is.'

The chocolate, Marty saw with relief, was still whole and wrapped.

'Why must you go back to the picnic? To see Hugo again?'

She shook her head dumbly.

'You still keen on marrying him?'

'My mother wishes it.'

'Why?'

'She wishes me to marry into the Wyldeck family.'

'Why?'

Marty burst into tears.

'Now look what I've done,' Tom said cheerfully. He broke the chocolate and gave her half. 'You must be starving, you didn't get your ice-cream by all accounts and I'll bet the sight of all those sheep and pigs roasting put you off your feed.'

Marty bit into the chocolate which tasted salty from the tears on her lips.

'My great-great-grandfather made his money shipping

31

slaves,' said Tom, his cheek full of chocolate, 'a thousand battened down in the bilge and if five-hundred died he still made a profit on the rest. My grandfather started a revolution, a bloody one, when he was Governor of the Pollyanna Islands. My old man's a compulsive gambler and my mother was in the illegitimate theatre. I wonder why your mother thinks the Wyldecks are a good family to marry into.'

'Do you think I ought to tell her—about your great-great-grandfather?'

'My dear girl you can't tell old people anything. They've got a different set of values.'

Marty was startled, she had never thought of her mother as old.

'Your mother would call it history, what all the best families have.'

It wasn't that old was such a bad thing to be, but it was a feeble and finished thing. 'My mother's not like that. She's—' Words failed her, as was to be expected.

'Well, what is she like?'

'She's not. Other people might be like *her* sometimes, a little, but she isn't like anyone.'

Tom yawned. 'I once tried to warn my father about a horse he was keen on for Aintree. I'd seen it dancing on its tail in the paddock and knew it would be a bad starter. He wouldn't listen, but he cut my allowance to stop me betting.'

If Marty were to tell her mother about the Wyldecks Nadia would listen carefully—she always gave Marty her best attention—and then she would withdraw, not every word, but certain ones, and the rest would fall to pieces.

'Perhaps your mother's thinking of us,' said Tom. 'Perhaps she thinks an injection of pure new blood into the Wyldeck stock would save us. Are you pure?'

'I don't know.'

'Purity's relative and flesh is grass anyway. Do you like otters?'

'I don't know any otters.'

'I'll show you some.' He rolled over and stood up, leaves and twigs clinging to his shoulders. 'There's a colony of them along the river-bank and they're fun to watch.'

'I must go back to the picnic.' If she didn't, Nadia would say, 'And so you left, you threw ice-cream at your host's son and left with no word,' and the shabby affair would be shaken out. 'I must apologise.'

'Hugo won't be there, he'll sulk for hours.'

'Then to your mother. I'll tell her I'm sorry—'

'For spoiling the plan? It hadn't a chance.' Tom hung his thumbs in his trousers pockets. 'You can't plan other people's lives.'

Nadia could, Nadia had worked at Marty's life. Other people might not know what they ought to do but Marty would always know—but would she ever be able to do it?

'It was so like me,' she said miserably. 'I ruined everything.'

'And neither your mother nor my mother nor anyone else's mother can change you. I'm glad, I respect a girl who throws ice-cream at her intended if he's not what she intended.' He took her arm with something of Hugo's ceremony. A long leaf was stuck into the thick of his hair, absurdly like an Indian's feather. 'Come on, Miss Meadowsweet, let's find the otters.'

*   *   *

Nadia told Peter that it was a symptom of the maladie Anglaise that children remained children so long.

'At seventeen I was not throwing ice-cream.'

'As Marty's only half-English it may have been her last fling.' Peter said gravely, 'I believe the pure-bred English girls throw ice-cream until they're twenty-one.'

'It is not a joke. Such capers are for children and in a year she will be a married woman. It will be necessary for her to develop very quickly.'

'Not all English women are developed by the time they

marry, some don't develop at all.' Peter made an elaborate gesture of deference. 'Of course it's different in France.'

'Of course,' Nadia agreed calmly. 'And a French woman still will be undeveloped when her husband so desires her.'

Neither bothered that Marty could hear the conversation, she was there in the room and would have had to stop up her ears to avoid hearing. That she would have done, but feared to turn their attention to her. There was some relief in being considered in absentia and in a kind of abeyance, as if the worst was done with and she might now improve. To be aware of her for a moment was to be aware of her insufficiency and that there was no end to it.

'So the Wyldeck project is off,' said Peter. 'I didn't think it a particularly good one.'

'It is a bad beginning but it is not the end.'

'I find George Wyldeck a bore and Minnie a tart—rather a stale tart.'

'You are not required to marry them.'

'Nor is Marty.'

'It is not the end,' Nadia said again and stretched up her arms so that her heavy bracelets slipped ringing from her wrists to her elbows. She was still beautiful and Peter still looked at her wryly, aware of his shortcomings. He had them, Marty knew, like everyone else. 'I am going to get Marty into the Wyldeck family,' said Nadia.

'I hope she'll be happy.'

He probably did, he was a kindly man and it simplified things if people were happy. And he did not need to worry because if anyone knew what constituted happiness for Marty surely Nadia did.

'She won't be penniless,' he said. 'In fact she'll be a catch so far as money is concerned.'

'For Tom, Dick or Harry to catch?'

There is Thomas Richard Henry Wyldeck, thought Marty, but she said nothing.

'For some opportunist to squander?'

'The money can be entailed.'

'Two fortunes are like two heads, better than one. Money should marry money, that is how to do the most good with it.'

*　　*　　*

That summer it was taken for granted that Marty and Hugo would marry. The Wyldecks gave parties and dances, the Prouts gave parties and dances and Marty and Hugo were planted in the thick of them.

Marty wondered why everyone was so pleased. She looked about her at the people laughing and dancing – surely they saw a golden future, a certain joy in this marriage which had been arranged. Why couldn't she see it too? What was so wrong and so lacking in her that she couldn't see it, let alone share it?

Hugo couldn't seem to see it either. He seldom laughed and he danced disobligingly and badly. Such conversation as he had with Marty was a kind of grumbling collusion, he was rebellious but he treated her less as a fellow rebel than the yoke he was being cumbered with.

'What do they think I am?' he asked her after his mother had suggested he take Marty on the lake by moonlight. 'A village Romeo?' And when his father referred to 'our two young people', he muttered, 'They may have given me birth but they haven't bought me.'

He and Marty did not meet except as their parents arranged. It was Nadia who asked Hugo over for tennis and Minnie Wyldeck who invited Marty for a spin in his new sports car and no one suggested that for an about-to-be-engaged couple it was in any way unusual. Marty did as she was asked and hoped she was doing right. She made no comparisons because her situation as Nadia's daughter had always been unique. She had no expectations of her own, but she had all Nadia's to come up to.

Fortunately these did not include a passionate or even a

customary courtship. Nadia set a few formal stages to the affair and required only that these should be accomplished.

Even at the parties and dances Hugo spent a merely nominal period with Marty. He kept his eye on someone or something else—his own reflection in a mirror preferably—and Marty grew accustomed to being overlooked. It was something of a relief, really it was the most she could hope from him.

Oddly enough, Tom Wyldeck helped, without meaning to, of course. He disapproved of the marriage scheme, he said it was doomed to failure sooner or later.

'Later than what?' Marty wanted to know.

'Too late. After you're married.'

'I'll cross that bridge when I come to it.' She was thinking that it wouldn't matter so much or it would matter differently and she certainly needn't worry herself about what would happen after she was married. 'I've got the ocean to cross first.'

'Oh Mrs. Prout,
There is no doubt
She'd drown herself, your daughter,
If you said she oughter,' chanted Tom.

He was at most of the Wyldecks' organised encounters, somewhere in the background, and Marty managed to slip into it with him after her token appearances with Hugo. Tom wasn't reassuring or sympathetic or kind, he didn't help what Marty was doing but he helped her and no one had done that before. His presence became important, second only in importance to the show or lack of a show which she put up. She counted on his being somewhere there, counted on his teasing, intolerance and mockery and on her own anger. Without his knowing and certainly without his wishing it, he gave her the heart to keep trying.

'Why don't you like my mother?'

'The question is, why do I like you, you silly little ghost? I

36

can't answer that.' He stared at her, his grin fixing. 'Whose ghost are you? Not yours—and not hers.'

'I don't know what you're talking about.'

'You've been born, you've got your own life and your own mind. You don't have to use your mother's any more.'

'If I did—if I *could*—it would be miles better than mine!'

Tom roared at her. 'If you're so darned inferior how can you know what she thinks? You only know what you think she thinks—did it strike you you could be wrong?'

There had to be an end to doubt and it enraged Marty that he should question what convictions she had. It also elated her a little to be free and able to be angry. She snatched at the chance.

'I'm not wrong! Oh, I can be, I can be wrong about everything—but not about her!'

'Then she's wrong about you!'

'You dare!' cried Marty. 'You dare to criticise her!'

'If she wants to marry you to Hugo she's dead wrong. You don't care for him and he doesn't care for you.'

'That isn't important!' Marty flung it out like a banner, it was what Nadia would have said.

'Of course it's important. It's all that is important, you silly little ghost!' Tom also was quite angry, his glasses misted over and he snatched them off and blinked his furiously watering eyes at her. 'You wouldn't care if my brother had two heads, would you? You'd marry him if she told you to!'

'Yes! Yes! Yes!' shouted Marty. 'I do everything she tells me!' and they glared at each other on a crest of rage.

Then Tom sighed. 'You couldn't haunt Hugo, you know.'

That made Marty feel sorry for herself and she burst into tears.

'You look awful when you cry,' Tom said unkindly.

*   *   *

The Wyldecks arranged a fancy dress ball to celebrate Hugo's twentieth birthday. They wished to announce his engagement to Marty on the same day.

'Ringing two birds in one party,' said Peter. 'Do I detect a certain retrenchment?'

'Don't be absurd. It is most suitable and it is time he proposed. You should not wear that shade of yellow, Marty, it makes you look as if you might not be altogether healthy.'

Peter asked Marty, 'Is the young man satisfactory from your point of view?' in the tone he might use to enquire about seating her on a train.

'If he asks me to marry him I shall say yes.'

'He should have asked you,' said Nadia. 'Three months is long enough to reach an understanding. Still, you will see to it. Tonight after the theatre, or if that is too public next Tuesday morning when you ride with him.'

'But how can I make him ask me?'

'Not make him, help him. You know how to do that?' Nadia raised her brows at Marty, then at Peter. It was not a question so much as a joke, the nearest they had ever come to a family joke. Marty couldn't smile, she looked into the lap of her yellow dress.

'It is inconceivable,' said Nadia, her brows suddenly descending, 'that I should have to teach my own daughter such things.'

'Inconceivable,' agreed Peter. 'Don't worry, she'll help young Wyldeck over the precipice when she's ready.'

He didn't understand, he still didn't, that it must be when Nadia was ready. Marty fiercely laced and unlaced her fingers in her yellow lap. If all men could be shown to be as artless and incomplete was there hope for her, even hope for Marty Prout with her desideratum?

Nadia tapped Peter on the shoulder. 'You mustn't suppose that I couldn't teach her.'

'I know damn well you could.'

'Or that I should have scruples. Women should know in their

bones or in their heads how to handle men and if they are not born with the knowledge they must learn.'

Or was it, Marty wondered, back where she started, Nadia's divine supremacy over creatures great and small?

'This knowledge is not nowadays always necessary for survival, but it is useful. A mother's duty is to see that her daughter has it—the hen also teaches her chicken to scratch in the dust.'

If she was so supreme, why was she here? The question surprised Marty. It had not occurred to her before, she hadn't been impious or modest enough to ask it.

Nadia turned to her. 'Tell me how it is between you. When you meet, what happens?'

'Nothing.'

'If you stand so, with your nose toute en droite and your chest like a policeman's, what should happen?'

'Perhaps young Wyldeck likes to cut a little ice,' suggested Peter.

'A man of your years might,' said Nadia, 'but a boy is tender and easily bruised. In marriage he believes he gives this great gift of himself and that what he takes in return is of minor importance. You must be warm, Marty, and receptive. Receive everything he offers, even the chair he pulls for you at table.' Nadia's eyes widened as her brows went up. 'Do you touch each other?'

Peter made a face, a comic one, but not to Marty. Perhaps he thought she couldn't or shouldn't share asides about Nadia.

'When we dance we do, and sometimes when we go for a drive. His car is very narrow—to lower the wind resistance.'

Nadia repeated, 'Wind resistance?' and discredit spread like ink on blotting-paper. 'Science is of no use.' She never laughed at Marty or lost her temper. Sometimes she showed impatience at the situation for developing or not developing, at words for being imprecise or at people for being misinformed. For Marty she reserved inveterate patience. 'I cannot tell you when or how or where you should touch him, but you must do it with both art and instinct. A man answers to your touch and this you will feel.'

She got up as she spoke and going to Peter brushed against his arm. Turning, she drew the tips of her fingers along his sleeve and over his wrist.

'It is not to make contact, and of course you are not so foolish as to lay claim, but to save him an effort of memory.'

She stood behind her husband, her breast lightly pressing his shoulder, and with feather touch followed the curve of his jacket collar down to his lapel. She did not look at him, she looked at Marty, holding her as she always did, spreadeagled to attention. Perhaps it was her gestures that seemed wrong, gestures of love without any love: without any consciousness even, just the same undiminished devotion to Marty that a trainer gives the creature he is trying to train.

'To remember what he has not yet experienced is beyond any man.'

For the first time in her life Marty felt that her mother might be wrong. And if she was, she was enormously and irredeemably wrong.

It was a shattering experience, everything fell apart, for every one person there were suddenly a thousand parts, for every animal and every bird a million, and every object was reduced to dust. Only Marty remained entire — being such a small grain there was no way to split her.

'You should also endeavour to remind the young man that when he takes you he will be taking a great deal of money.'

There was no need for Nadia to shake out the folds of her dress as she moved away, she had already dropped Peter from her little finger.

'Few girls nowadays have such a *dot*. Money is the only experience which can be remembered in advance.'

*   *   *

Hugo looked splendid in his fancy dress. He wore the full ceremonials of an officer of the 11th Hussars and the contrast between him and Tom was so meticulous that Marty was suspicious of it.

'Did you have to wear that?' she asked Tom.

The ruff of his baggy clown's costume kept riding up to his ears. He battered it down, winking his pebble lenses at her. 'It's traditional for a mountebank.'

After all, they were brothers, that should have given them some relevance. But whereas Hugo was radiant with the innocent strength that every mother likes to see in her son, Tom was a half-licked cub, grubby and shapeless.

'Why wear *that* costume? It's most unbecoming,' said Marty.

'Appropriate though.'

'Why? You're not a clown. But you couldn't compete with Hugo, could you? You'd rather go to the other extreme and dress up as what you know you're not and be quite, quite safe. That's conceited and cowardly.'

'*You* shouldn't have come as nobody's ghost.'

They glared and turned their backs. It wasn't the first tiff they had had, they sparked each other off and to Marty that was important. After the cold fishiness of Hugo it was heart-warming. She and Tom did not prolong their differences, they met days or minutes after as if nothing had happened – except that they seemed to have got a little further on, though what with or what to Marty had no idea.

Minnie Wyldeck beckoned to her. 'Thank goodness you don't look any different dear, in your costume. I find it so tiresome trying to place people. What are you – Alice in Wonderland?'

'No, Helen of Troy. I'm supposed to have a chignon but it keeps slipping.'

'Don't worry about that now, I want you and Hugo to open the dancing.'

Marty looked at the circling couples. 'They're dancing already.'

'Not officially. The band has orders not to strike up properly until I give the signal. That will be when Hugo leads you on to the floor.'

'He hasn't asked me to dance with him.'

'He will.'

When Minnie Wyldeck rose to her rotund full height of four feet ten inches the band stopped playing at once and everyone looked round. Perhaps she had acquired the knack of commanding attention in the theatre. She snapped her fingers and the officer of Hussars came reluctantly.

'Go on boy, lead her out.' Minnie tweaked his gold frogging. 'It's your privilege as a courting couple.'

Hugo clicked his heels and bowed stiffly from the waist. He hitched Marty's hand high in his and marched on to the dance floor. Marty was forced to go, she didn't have a moment to fix her chignon before becoming the cynosure of all eyes.

The conductor was glad to see them and every man in the orchestra took up his instrument as if about to break a fast. Minnie gave the signal and they were all precipitated into a rumba.

Hugo said nothing but the chin strap of his plumed hat pressed hard under his lip, it was a furry hat and probably hot. His white gloves were damp to Marty's touch. In a way she felt sorry for him, he had his own idea of himself to live up to and it must be so terribly explicit. She knew that she didn't come up to his idea of a wife for himself, but his idea stood no chance beside her mother's. The priorities remained the same and there could be only one failure.

A warm drop fell on her arm. She should be receptive of everything, even of the chair he offered her, certainly she should receive the sweat of his brow.

After the rumba the orchestra dived without pause into a lively foxtrot. The heat was getting personal. Someone opened a window but Minnie Wyldeck immediately made her commanding gesture and it was shut again.

'Why did she do that?' cried Marty.

'We've no intention of being left with gallons of ice-cream on our hands,' Hugo said grimly. He whirled Marty so fast about that they bumped into the next couple. Marty felt something tumble down her back, and seem to get mixed up with their feet. She had an unpleasant sensation of kicking something soft and lively.

'What's that?' Hugo tried to look down.

'I think I've dropped something—'

A girl shrieked 'Oh look—a mouse!' and there was pandemonium, screams and shouts and stamping and a panic rush of girls to break out of the solid sea of dancers.

'It's a rat!'

'It's a mole!'

'It's dead—'

'It's my hair-piece,' said Marty. 'Let me get it, please.'

But Hugo held her with a grip of iron. 'Keep dancing!'

She tried to stand still, he tightened his arm round her waist and lifted her as if she were a doll. Someone else picked up her chignon and they made great play of pretending that it was a small savage animal. Amid applause and laughter it was finally thrown out into the night.

Then, 'I'm damned if I'll marry you,' he said and didn't wait even to escort her off the floor.

Marty sought breathing space, physical and mental, in the garden. She also looked for her chignon. She didn't want it, she didn't want to see it again, but it had been a temporary part of her and she wasn't going to leave it among the Wyldeck rose-bushes for the gardeners to find. She knew she wouldn't be coming here again. It was all over, not only because Hugo would be damned if he'd marry her but because she had reached a point of return only. It must be. She certainly couldn't go any further nor could she stay where she was and as she was.

Somehow she had to get back, a long way back to where she had started. There was a choice once and she made the wrong one. It wasn't too late to make another.

She was still searching and getting scratched by thorns when Tom found her.

'What are you up to, Miss Meadowsweet?'

'I'm looking for my hair.'

'What?'

'It's not really mine. I didn't grow it but I was wearing it and someone put it out of the window.'

'Tell me about it.'

Marty told him about the dancing and her chignon falling off and people pretending it was an animal.

'Hugo swore he wouldn't marry me.'

'You can't blame him. If you throw ice-cream and hair at him before you're engaged what can he expect when you're married?'

'It's all over. I shall tell my mother but I shan't tell her why. I can't!'

'You'll get in a frightful mess walking about those beds. They've just been mulched.'

'I'm looking for my chignon.'

'Perhaps it's run to its burrow.'

'You're crude!'

'I say, do be careful of those roses, you're breaking off the buds—'

'Bother your buds!' Marty wrung a Frau Karl Druchski by its neck and tore it to pieces. 'I'll never set foot in this place again!' A sweet peppery smell of torn petals came from her fingers.

Tom said thoughtfully, 'You could always marry me.'

'Always?' She couldn't think of anything else to say. She still wanted to be angry, she still was angry.

'I'm available. A point in my favour so far as you're concerned is that I'm a Wyldeck.'

'But you don't love me!'

'Don't I?'

They stared at each other, then Marty stamped her foot so furiously that soft earth from the flowerbed went into her shoe.

'You're not funny!'

'You may be right,' said Tom, 'about love, I mean. I'd have to find out what it entails. People do sound off so about it. "Falling" in love now—' he looked at her soberly—'does it have to be thumping? Or can you work into it steady and quiet like a capsid bug into an apple?'

Marty didn't care for the image but she could see that he wasn't joking. He was asking—oh he wouldn't accept an answer if she came up with one, but he really was asking in a rhetorical way.

'One's got to be capable—constitutionally I mean. Some people aren't built that way and they never get into it, thumping or steady. Perhaps I shan't. On the other hand—' his lenses twinkled at her—'perhaps I have.'

'Oh dear,' said Marty.

'There never was the remotest chance of you getting to be Mrs. Hugo, you know.'

'Yes there was, my mother wanted it and there was every chance.'

'Not a snowball's in hell. So I didn't worry,' said Tom cheerfully. Somehow they both appreciated that it was beside the point that she had been prepared to marry Hugo who certainly didn't love her. 'I'd have done something if there had been.'

'What would you have done?'

'Thrown ice-cream and hair at Hugo probably.'

Marty cried, 'You don't love me, of course you don't!'

Tom said huffily, 'I suppose you think I'm not capable of it.'

Marty shook her head. The scorn had been for herself, not him. She had caught herself hoping, it seemed she was incurably hopeful. Here she was, after everything that had happened to

45

her, had been happening for eighteen long years, snatching at the same straw. She was only doing as she always had done, hoping to come up to expectation. Only now it was Tom's expectation.

'You haven't said how you feel about me.'

His expectation would be entirely different from her mother's but would it be any easier to come up to? Only if it were very much less, and what right had she to hope that?

'I don't know.'

'Well I'm ready to risk it. I'd rather risk it with you than be certain with anyone else.' He pushed up his glasses and blinked at her. 'It'll do for a start.'

It was he who said so, he who wanted to start. He was willing to take what she was, as a humble beginning.

She sighed. 'I'll never be any different.'

'I don't want you to be.'

'But I shan't improve, this is the best I can be. My mother's always waiting for me to be what I really am—' Marty took off her shoe and emptied out the earth—'and I've never been able to be anything.'

'I don't want you different,' said Tom again. 'I like you as you are, when you are—which is when you're with me.'

Did he know what he was saying? She had marvelled at his assurance and shaken her head over it, diametrically opposed as he was to all Nadia's principles. Could she trust him, could she trust anyone to want only what she could give?

'When you're not with me you're nobody's ghost. I reckon I can turn you into your own flesh and blood.'

Marty had scarcely any idea what he meant but she thought he could do it. Moreover, she thought it was what she needed— she needed practically everything.

'You're not God, Tom Wyldeck!'

'Sometimes I am, I reckon we all are sometimes,' he said cheerfully.

It was a foolish blasphemous thing to say and she should at

least have been annoyed, on several counts she should have been really angry. She tried, she said, 'When was *I* last God?'

'Probably at this minute, you're treading on a worm.'

She stepped too hurriedly off the flower-bed and he caught and steadied her. His plain bun face was neither good nor God-like but she found it sustaining. She was absolutely sustained and knew what he meant about her being nobody's ghost. She knew, too, about making her her own flesh and blood.

Then he said, 'Marrying into the Wyldecks is what your mother wants, isn't it?'

Perhaps he said that to help himself, perhaps to help Marty, or perhaps just to tease—his teasing used to help her once.

Not any more. Why he said it, or how, or whether he said it at all didn't help either of them because Marty would have remembered it herself sooner or later.

She stood up to him as stiff as a poker. 'I can't marry you.'

'Why not?'

'Because I won't have what she wants as a reason for anything I do. I won't ever have that again.'

'Bravo, little ghost!' Smiling, he rocked her rigid shoulders. 'Of course you must have your own reasons for marrying me.'

'I have that one for not marrying you,' said Marty.

*　　*　　*

In the afternoons there were always callers, certain people came on certain afternoons and Marty supposed they kept to a rota. People of her mother's age and persuasions—they wouldn't come at all if they were not of Nadia's persuasions—were comfortable only within limits.

Marty blamed them for that. After two weeks of the bell ringing and the knocker knocking between three o'clock and four, never before and never after, after opening it to the faces, old and lapsed and delicate, of Delbanco and Earlbeck and Fischer and Dutt, and the posturing green back of Sammy

47

Crisp, she blamed them quite bitterly. After two weeks she stopped going to the door and it was left on the latch for them to let themselves in.

There was no quicker or more arbitrary way of losing thirty solid years than by returning to the house of her childhood. After two weeks the life which had not begun until she left this house had gone. When she came back, thirty years of marriage lost their substance and occurred to her as if from a dream or a book once read.

Of course it wasn't only those frail old creatures ineluctably turning up every afternoon who took away her substance: there was the house of her childhood which had hardly changed, and there was Nadia. And time did not stand still, it continued to move at the same rate. The morning still waited at ten. Having dressed and breakfasted and seen the papers there was nothing to do. Marty found herself with her forehead against the window, where she used to wait as a child when waiting was the best thing she could do—the happiest, anyway—before she tried and as likely as not failed.

She was waiting now to see if it would be a fine day and if the wood-doves still came and was there cosy white steam still over the gas coolers. One might say that the only difference was in her mirror. She had become fat, a fat middleaged stranger with a young Marty peeping out like the young of a kangaroo peeping out of its pouch.

Nadia had retained enough of her essentials to make her look not different, but more like herself. She still had the shape of her abundant hair and the breadth of her shoulders, and her voice and the movements of her hands had all their old capacity. She was eighty years old and age could not crack her.

Until ten-thirty she sat at her dressing-table putting back a heightened version of her face.

'As a woman grows older she should devote more time to her appearance.'

Marty said, 'There's such a thing as growing old gracefully.'

48

'My dear, forgive me, but is that what you claim to be doing?'

Smiling, she patted rouge under her cheekbones. Marty smiled too. Did she really think she would be forgiven for the asking?

'I know that this is a difficult time for you.'

'I can't live alone.'

'One gets used to it. But there is no need, we are mother and daughter, we are both widows and this house is large. It would be foolish to keep separate establishments.'

Their reflections smiled back, Nadia's at Marty's, Marty's at herself. Nadia could not frighten her now. All that she could do was to remind Marty of the process. And this house could do as much: here were the corners she had gone to in her extremity, the shadows she had watched and envied and the wood and fabrics, china and glass that were more Nadia than her own flesh and blood.

'I had been expecting you.' With a deft hand Nadia restored the pure black arches of her brows.

'You mean you expected Eric to die?'

'Men do not live as long as women and naturally I hoped that you would come home.'

'This hasn't been my home for thirty years.'

'He did not deserve you. He should have married an ordinary creature like himself.'

'I am an ordinary creature. We were well-matched, if matching is what's needed.'

'It is not, of course,' said Nadia, 'and he should perhaps have married someone superficially brilliant. But I am not interested in his *mésalliance*, only in yours.'

Eric used to roar when Nadia's name was mentioned, a spontaneous bellow of alarm. He really was intimidated although he made a joke of it. Once he rounded on Marty saying, 'If I find one particle of her in you I'll be gone like a shot from a gun', and Marty had almost told him how she had searched for it in

D

herself in vain. Almost, not quite. He would have resented having to re-think her at their time of life.

'I may go abroad,' she said.

'I was about to suggest it.' Nadia was edifying to watch. She faithfully interpreted her face feature by feature. Too faithfully — that was her mistake, thought Marty, people didn't look so like themselves. 'You could go to your cousin in Dijon.'

'Whatever would I do in Dijon?'

'You could see a dressmaker and go to the hairdresser. Then there is your skin, it is so sad.' Nadia leaned to the mirror and stared into it past her own reflection to Marty's. 'Surtout there is your figure, you must have a masseuse and a diet. For years you have eaten more than you need, you have tried to console yourself with food.'

'Eric and I were happy!'

'One must be thankful you did not descend to keeping little dogs.' Nadia used tweezers to pluck a bristle from her lip.

'Eric was my consolation. He gave me everything he could.'

'And you were content? Because if you were, the fault was yours for wanting so little.'

'So little?' Marty spun Nadia round, face to unfinished face. 'I wanted heaven and earth. You made sure I'd never be content with less.'

Nadia touched Marty's cheek with her tweezers. 'So many enlarged pores — you who had a skin like pearl.'

True, Marty enjoyed food. She had to. Eric liked big solid meals and if she couldn't enjoy them with him their lives wouldn't have been worth living.

'You're putting it on, old girl,' he used to say admiringly. Sometimes she thought that the meal table was their marriage bed and the puddings and pies, the silverside and dumplings, the white bread and black fruit cake, the gammon rashers and Belgian buns they ate together were sex at a remove.

Here I am now, she said to herself, all passion spent, and she picked up her breakfast tray and took it to the kitchen.

'What's this?' she said to the housekeeper.

'Black tea, fruit juice, Melba toast.'

'Well the joke's over, I want something to eat.'

'I understood that you were going to diet.'

'Then you misunderstood. I'm having bacon and eggs, coffee with cream and buttered toast and marmalade.' Marty went to the fridge. 'I'll see to it myself if you'll let me use your kitchen.'

'That won't be necessary. I'll attend to it immediately.'

Nadia's housekeeper was young and depersonalised. So was the food she prepared. Marty hadn't tasted a good baked potato or a melting piecrust since she came back. The vegetables were tiny and immature—petits pois and button sprouts—unidentifiable by taste or so crisp that they exploded on the tongue.

Marty watched her trim off the rinds, this woman made fried eggs and bacon look like a milliner's confection.

'Those rashers must have come from the pig's tail. You should get a decent bit of back.'

'Mrs. Prout never touches this sort of thing.'

'I'll have three as they're so small.'

The housekeeper chose a frying-pan as if it were an expensive and tricky piece of apparatus. Coraline, the daily help, was on her knees pushing a scrubbing brush over the floor.

Marty said to her, 'My husband liked me as I am.'

'Yeh.'

'He liked big things. Big women, big appetites.' Marty rubbed her cheek. 'Big pores.'

'Yeh.'

'I don't eat for consolation, I'm not disappointed. It's not as if I'm a goose thinking I ought to be a swan. I'm not a talking stomach either.'

'Yeh.'

'Bread and jam, oil and water, flesh and the spirit, what I think of myself can't be solaced in my stomach.'

'Yeh.'

Marty stepped back from the grey sudsy tide Coraline was

bringing up to her feet. 'They should get you a squeeze-mop for that job. People don't have to go on their knees nowadays, not even to God.'

Coraline's skin was the colour of Guinness. The pupils of her eyes were the same rich velvet, the whites stained as if the pigmentation was too strong to be kept out. When asked where she came from she said 'Siddam', which could equally well be in South East London or Africa. The round bones at the base of her neck were no bigger than pebbles.

'You could do with more flesh on you.'

'Yeh.'

'Don't you ever say anything else?'

Coraline turned her head. Her grin was brief and brilliant as a sabre flash. 'Yeh.'

'The girl's arms are like sticks,' Marty said to the housekeeper.

'But she's thickening round the middle.'

'What do you mean?'

'I mean there's a brown bun in the oven.'

'What?' Marty was more affronted by the culinary turn of phrase than shocked by the information.

'You'll want two eggs I suppose?'

'She's only a child herself—and not married!'

'She doesn't know who the father is.'

'That's terrible!'

'It's typical,' said the housekeeper. 'Two eggs?'

Marty put her hand on the girl's shoulder and halted the wide whispering sweep of the scrubbing-brush. 'Is it true?'

'Yeh.'

'Is it true what she's saying? That you're pregnant?'

Coraline's grin split her face. 'Yeh.'

'Ask her if she's President of the United States,' suggested the housekeeper, 'and she'll say the same.'

'Coraline, listen to me. Are you going to have a baby?' Marty cradled her arms and rocked them. 'A baby!'

Coraline laughed. She enjoyed the joke, parting her pointed

white teeth to show her pointed pink tongue dodging about behind them. 'Bibby, yeh!'

'It stands to reason,' said the housekeeper, 'if that's all she ever says.'

'Does my mother know?'

'It was she who pointed it out to me.'

'What does she say?'

'We won't discuss it.' With a beautiful movement she broke an egg and dropped it from the palm of her hand into the lightly humming pan. 'Not a very savoury subject.'

Marty made up her mind that Nadia would discuss it with her; savoury or not, it was preferable to any other subject they were likely to discuss.

'How old are you, Coraline?'

'Bibby!' Laughing and shaking her head over the joke Coraline climbed to her feet. There was a definite clumsiness about her movements and her small stomach jutted ruthlessly.

'Coraline! I asked how old you are.'

She looked at Marty with her lips pursed, tasting the fun of the word 'bibby'. An element of thought, very slight, flickered over her smooth brow. She said 'Fifteen', and nodded. 'Yeh.'

'My God,' said Marty, 'you little fool.'

Coraline cradled the scrubbing-brush to her chest and rocked her arms. 'Bibby!'

'Hasn't she any parents?'

'You should ask Mrs. Prout,' said the housekeeper. 'She engaged her.'

'I shall.' Marty picked up her plate of frilly plastic eggs and bacon. 'Is there no fried bread?'

'The carbohydrates in a slice of fried bread are in an inverse ratio to the nutritional value and with a heavy calorie intake of three rashers of bacon I should have thought you'd relate your activity foods to what you expect to be doing and eating the rest of the day.' When the housekeeper sighed something very

53

stiff rustled in sympathy. 'But of course if you really think you should—'

'Oh never mind,' said Marty, thinking it would probably have looked like a bit of uncut moquette anyway. She took her plate up to Nadia's room.

She hadn't forgotten anything about Nadia so shouldn't have been surprised by her attitude. But she still had the right to be shocked by it.

'So when she can no longer work you'll just sack her?'

'It will be quite soon,' said Nadia. 'She does little enough and I cannot afford to have her do less.'

'What will become of her?'

'The Welfare State will provide.'

'Could she get a maternity grant? Has she paid enough contributions to be in benefit? She's only a child, fifteen years old—'

'My dear, I don't pay insurance for her. She costs enough as it is. I employ her to keep Miss Hargreaves happy. Poor Miss Hargreaves likes to think that someone else does the rough work. Actually,' Nadia powdered into the hollows of her neck, 'she does most of it herself and pride is served because she can claim that her standards don't allow her to be content with what the girl does. Coraline is employed on a casual basis, no one could be more casual as to the amount of work she does.'

'But she must have someone to turn to! What about her parents?'

'By all means let her turn to them.'

'Are you sure that she has parents?'

'My dear, if you must eat breakfast on this scale will you please do so elsewhere? I should certainly prefer you not to bring it here in order *not* to eat it.'

Marty took a forkful of egg. Now that it had gone cold it also tasted like plastic. She was thinking that someone should find out about Coraline.

*   *   *

LA MATIÈRE

The girl lived in a Victorian terrace house in an area scheduled for redevelopment. She shared a room with an old woman and a married couple. They had pinned sheets of newspaper over a clothes-line down the middle. Coraline and the old woman lived on one side, the man and wife on the other.

The old woman's name was O'Shaughnessy, she and Coraline both came from Port of Spain but seemed not to be related. When Marty called she was greeted with expansive gestures and cracking great smiles and made much of. The minute she set foot on Coraline's side of the newspaper she felt like one of their household gods, omnipotent and kiddable.

The old woman installed her in a huge cane chair, in fact it was the only chair. The space just took a camp bed and a dreadfully uncomfortable-looking ottoman—Marty hoped Coraline didn't sleep on it—a tin trunk, a meat safe, a gas-ring in a biscuit tin and a brass fish kettle. The dividing newspaper ended in the middle of the fireplace and Marty wondered if each side burned their own coal at either end of the grate. The place was clean, a nice smell came from a bundle of brown vegetables like thumbs.

'Is Coraline's name O'Shaughnessy too?' asked Marty.

'Bless you, my husband was an Irish captain and died before ever I got here.'

There was an element of kidding about the way the old woman practically curtsied to Marty, spreading her skirts round her like a big coloured pancake.

Coraline giggled. 'Antie Nessy.'

'You hear what she calls me? I don't know how I come by that girl.' She unpinned a square of the newspaper wall and called through, 'We have a visitor *if* you please,' and when she turned her pride was in Marty. 'You Coraline stand up, don't lie about in front of Missis Prout.'

'I'm not Mrs. Prout, I'm her daughter. And I'm here because Coraline's in trouble.'

'She ain't never been out of it.'

'What about her parents? Where are they?'

'Parents?' The old woman danced her fingers in the air round Marty's hat in a rush of admiration. 'She never had no parents.'

'Mrs. O'Shaughnessy, we're not having that Topsy stuff. The person with the first responsibility to Coraline is her mother. Is she in Trinidad or is she dead?'

'Coraline ain't had no mother. You got Missis Prout, Coraline ain't never had a mother like that.'

'It doesn't matter what she was like, where is she now?'

'That's a rare pretty hat,' said Mrs. O'Shaughnessy reverently. 'Certainly a woman bore this Coraline and she stayed around for a while. But not like Missis Prout. She pretty soon upped and went.'

'I wish you'd sit down.' They upset Marty, the old woman swaying and creaking in her huge bright skirts and the girl holding her stomach as if it were a small melon. But it was their home and she requested them, 'Please won't you both sit down?'

The old woman wasn't ready to, she wanted to look round Marty and Coraline obviously took her cue from her.

'I hear Missis Prout's a fine lady.'

They were smiling, there was no stopping Mrs. O'Shaughnessy's smile. Her face had shaped to it over a lifetime. But why so pleased? Why were they so pleased with Marty? Someone laughed on the other side of the newspaper, a titter that broke out again and again. So much pleasure made Marty uneasy.

'Coraline's only got you then, Mrs. O'Shaughnessy?'

'This Coraline got what's inside her and that's all she got.'

Coraline giggled and Marty said, 'Forgive me, I must ask you, is she simple in the head?'

'Simple, is it?' Mrs. O'Shaughnessy's black lips still smiled but her eyes uncrinkled. 'Don't mistake this girl, Missis Prout's daughter. She wasn't bred up but she's got wits working for her all the time. Yes, once she got born I reckon she had to have wits to get her her mother's milk.' The laughter in the other half of the room vexed her.

She beat on the newspaper crying, 'Bone ignorant, you Selwyns!'

'What's to become of her?'

'She'll do as she is.'

'But she won't be as she is in a month or two's time!'

'You said that well.' The old woman was all white teeth and white eyes and bright skirts shaking.

Everyone was laughing, Mrs. O'Shaughnessy, Coraline, the pair on the other side of the newspaper. Marty thought incredulously if this is fun what are they like when they really enjoy themselves?

She got up and gave Coraline an ungentle push backwards on to the camp bed.

'Listen to me, what are you going to do when your time comes?'

'My time come.'

'When the baby comes!'

Coraline sprawled across the bed, spider-black and glittering with laughter. 'I'll give it away!'

'I hear Missis Prout's a very titled lady, all alone in twenty-five rooms, or was until her only daughter came to live. Both widow ladies I hear, like me—that I don't hear!' Shaking, Mrs. O'Shaughnessy offered Marty the joke on her two pink palms.

Coraline too held out her hands. 'I'll give the bibby to Missis Prout.'

★   ★   ★

Nadia couldn't think what Marty was worrying about. The girl would be looked after, there were people who made it their business.

'Business?'

'Yes, business, because that's the way to get things done. You don't imagine this is an isolated case or that you are the first to

57

think of it? There are thousands of such girls and they don't have to go out with begging bowls. Everything is provided.'

'What is provided? The bare necessities for them to deliver their babies.'

'That, after all, is what they want — to deliver them into someone else's hands.'

'Coraline herself has been handed round like a hot potato. She's still a child.'

'She's not our responsibility.'

'I think she is. They're all our responsibility, all the young ones are the responsibility of all the older ones. Who else? Welfare State isn't who, it's what. Things can't be answerable for people.'

'It's a pity you have no child of your own.'

'Would it have been such a blessing?'

'It would have been better than someone else's child. Eh bien, you have no child and now no husband. If you can interest yourself in welfare work it will be quite suitable.' Nadia, who sometimes indulged herself in the old-fashioned way, dipped a corner of her brioche into her coffee. 'On committees you meet with useful people, provided, of course, you join the right ones. I shall speak to Fabia Earlbeck.'

'Useful for what?'

'You are still a relatively young woman —'

'Relative to what?'

'Will you let me finish? You see, you are edgy and fretful since you lost your prospect. You never did yourself justice, but now you shall —'

'I don't think the girl should be on her knees scrubbing floors and carrying heavy pails of water.'

'Then she had better go.'

'You'd turn her adrift?'

'I shall stop paying her for what she does not do. I was afraid that work and the girl were strangers but I hoped she might be good for something — apart from what she has so obviously been good for,' Nadia said, smiling. 'You know, you would find a touch of politics stimulating. I am thinking not of Parliamentary or Government—this is so much place-seeking—but of fringe affairs. Ambrose Dutt is Chairman of Societies for integration or segregation, I am not sure which, but if race relations are important to you it is there you should start.'

'It's never been necessary for you to know me,' said Marty, 'or to look at me. It's never been possible for you to see past your blinding great vision of yourself.'

Nadia's eyes widened, she inclined her head slightly as if acknowledging half a point.

'I'm a plain ordinary woman without ambition or ideas. You'd better accept that. I know it wounds your vanity to have a plain ordinary daughter but we've neither of us got so much time left to live with the fact.'

'You have been your own enemy. You have fought to lose and your greatest loss was the marriage you made. This we both know.' Nadia gave an intimation of a sigh which she wouldn't have allowed herself once. 'It's been a long battle, now it must be ended.'

'It's not a battle! This is me, *my* self, not an extension of yours. Oh don't grieve,' said Marty, 'there really isn't anything of you in me.'

Someone was singing. Out on the front porch Coraline lifted her reedy voice as she washed the step. Rejoicing? What had she to rejoice at, she wasn't even assured of a place on Mrs. O'Shaughnessy's side of the newspaper.

They listened. Marty tried to discover something about Coraline, something, anything, that could be pinned on her. There was the baby, that should be enough to pin on any girl, but already it seemed to exist of itself. That hump in her stomach looked lonely.

Nadia probably wasn't listening. In the strong morning light the colours laid on her face did not cohere, each stood out like the colours on a flag. She stretched out her hand to Marty.

Marty couldn't remember the last time she had touched her mother. In childhood she had longed to and lived in dread that she might do it by accident. They always stopped short of actual contact, even when they met after long absence they only made the gesture, an inch apart, of touching their cheeks together.

Marty did not know what to do about the hand, she could not ignore it. She had quite consciously to think what she would have done had it been someone else's. Awkwardly she moved to take it.

'When did you last go to Mass?' said Nadia.

'I haven't been for years.'

'Will you come with me?'

It was the last thing Marty expected. Nadia was holding and almost dragging at her hand, gripping Marty's fingers between her rings.

'We can go to Confession together.'

'You and I?'

'You should start by having a little religion again.'

'You and I confessing the same sins? Is that how you see it?'

'I see that it will help you make a new beginning.'

'You're always trying to get me in somewhere.' Marty held up their clasped hands and considered them as if they were a rarity, as indeed they were. 'Do you think we share our sins, yours at the back of mine and mine at the bottom of yours? I'm afraid you won't have any better luck getting me into Heaven.'

'My sins are my own and I shall answer for them.'

Nadia released Marty's hand and it was left in the air with the marks of Nadia's rings reddening across the fingers. The hand was unremarkable really, except when looked at as a little fat blind white beast. Really it was best not looked at at all.

'I shall go home tomorrow and take Coraline with me. To live.'

Nadia paused with her coffee cup halfway to her lips. 'Why?'

'She has nowhere else to go.'

'Do you like this girl?'

Marty didn't particularly. When she thought of Coraline's skinny black arms and legs and little swollen ball in the middle she was always reminded of a spider.

'I'm going to see that she has her baby and learns how to bring it up decently.'

'You will teach her?'

'It's not necessary to give birth to know how to take care of a child.'

'And then?' Nadia put her cup to her lips. After all, it didn't amount to much more than a pause in a sip of coffee. 'You and the girl will live together?'

'I'm going to be responsible for her, I'm going to make her—' Marty had intended to say 'happy', but Coraline was singing out on the porch. 'I'll make a woman of her.'

Almost an International Incident

'Six o'clock. We'd have been in Rimini now.'

'And I'd be in my bath. Did you know there's only one bagno to each floor? Five times I tried the door on ours and each time a different voice was singing "Carmen".'

'Wouldn't we, Harold? Wouldn't we have been in Rimini?'

'Men — at least I think they were — singing the Toreador song, but the last one sounded high and reedy.'

'It was the same guy washing himself away.'

'I know it was Rimini we'd have been because I cast my travel diary according to the itinerary and after lunch I was all set to write up the Mandrioli Pass.'

'The steam was coming out of the keyhole. I tell you that door was wet *through*.'

'Right after we left Florence I knew we wouldn't get over those hills.'

'When we were riding down from Lenslebourg the bus gave a shudder right on the edge of one of those drops and seemed to lose herself. An old Buick I had did that, just rolled over and died.'

'The guy's a lousy driver.'

'Wouldn't you expect them to have more than one bathroom on each floor? I mean, it's styled a hotel, not a pensione.'

'I guess we're lucky to be here without booking or anything.'

'Did we know the bus was going to break down? We booked a tour, not a mosey-round.'

'I expressed myself before we started. "This is a cheap package," I said to Harold, "and it'll be trimmed to the bone, there's no way else they can do it for the price", and he said, "So long as they provide the fundamentals", and I said, "What we call fundamental they call fancy".'

'Well I'm glad to be here. It's an opportunity we would have missed if that cotter-pin hadn't broken.'

'Opportunity for what?'

'For seeing this place which is an unscheduled stop. We never would have known it existed. We'd have rushed on by—and for what?'

'For a bath at the Bellavista.'

'Everyone gets to Rimini. We've got the chance to experience some place else and I think we should make the most of it.'

Pearl Rubinsky thought so too. She and Bennet always agreed about these things, the first time she ever heard Ben he was voicing her thoughts.

'Did you see those holes in the rock? People are living in them. Real troglodytes!'

'The water in the whisky tastes like real river,' said Vic Farrar.

'We came on this trip to see something outside ourselves and I'd say this place is right outside us.'

Plump Wilma Borg said it wasn't what she came for.

'We've a real chance to get to know people. The danger as I see it is of being encapsulated in that bus and never contacting reality.'

'I think it's nice stopping over in the mountains,' said Pearl. 'Everyone else will be down at Rimini.'

'You making it out some kind of privilege, Pearl?'

'Not to be in Rimini now? *Not* drinking at Morissey's?'

'Give me the Bellavista any time.'

'Pearl, don't put words in my mouth!' Bennet was pink and a little mortified. 'Don't do that, Pearl, it's how wars are started.'

'Let's go and eat.' Vic picked up a handful of his wife's long hair, he often invited her with a tug. She made no objection, shook her hair back on her shoulders when he let go and looked with her pale eyes askew—Bennet had said he felt he wanted to align them for her. 'What are they giving us for dinner?'

'String soup in a tureen painted with the story of the Fall.'

When Vic and Nell Farrar went to find the dining-room the others stopped talking generally among themselves. Ben worried because Pearl's ankles were puffy. He made her sit down so that he could touch them and gauge her discomfort.

Wilma Borg talked to the Harold Harpers, Mrs. Harold was scoring through and through 'FRIDAY—Rimini' in her travel diary. It was no longer possible to know what they were thinking, or rather it was not possible to stop them thinking the wrong thing.

'They don't want,' Pearl said sadly, 'they just don't.'

'Never mind about them. Are *you* all right?'

'I'm fine.' She was seven months pregnant and they had debated exhaustively whether they should come on this trip. But it would be years before they could contemplate it again. 'We'll go out tonight, won't we?'

'Maybe you should rest with your feet on a pillow.'

'Ben, we did say we'd never let it restrict us—'

'This side of risk I said, Pearl.'

'My ankles will be down in the morning, they always are.'

Vic Farrar had carried his whisky into the dining-room. The bottle stood bald and functional beside the wicker-covered Chianti flask. Nell Farrar was composedly eating spaghetti and Vic was trying to snatch the ends of it out of her mouth.

'I wish he wouldn't horse around,' muttered Pearl.

'He drinks too much.'

They wanted to sit over away from the Farrars but Vic beckoned them.

'Come on, you two, this is where they cook the string and save the chicken but I've had them untie the knots first.'

Bennet and Pearl sat down at the next table and Bennet put up the menu between themselves and the Farrars. 'Someone should tell him it reflects on us all.'

'But not you, he's older than you. Also he's bigger. Harold Harper should speak to him.'

'Or Wilma.' They smiled at each other. Wilma Borg was bigger than Vic.

Pearl felt hungry, she usually did now, and there were savoury smells from the kitchen which opened out of the dining-room, and from the windows which opened on the piazza came a smell more pungent which enlivened senses deeper than those of taste. She asked Bennet if he could smell the olives.

He sniffed judiciously. 'I didn't think olive trees smelt.'

'They do, I know they do. I know that smell from way back, it seems like from before I was born.' Pearl said wonderingly, 'My great-grandmother was Italian. Do you think it could be in my blood? And that's why I feel at home? I do, Ben, I feel I belong here.'

'It's well known, Pearl, that women in your condition have queer fancies.'

'This is absolutely nothing to do with my condition, this is with me, Pearl Rubinsky, Pearl Patten that was, or just Pearl or just that was and am and will be again when the condition's over.'

'I'm glad—'

'Also,' said Pearl, really liking the place—the check tables and green vines and even the cheap pictures of big-breasted girls—as she knew she wouldn't like any other place on the trip and as she would probably never be able to like any other place

again, 'I feel that the people here are my friends. They may be
more than that, I'm not sure whether it's a blood-tie—'

'Hey,' cried Vic, 'Nell's going to show how the contadini
drink wine!'

Nell picked up his whisky-bottle and put it under her chair.

'Wine for my wife—in a goat-skin!'

'Signor, we have no goats.'

'It was a joke,' Pearl said, gently smiling to the girl who was
serving them.

The girl looked into Pearl's eyes and the frown vanished from
between her own. She set down the great tureen which she
carried from table to table and asked pleadingly, 'Signora, is
everything all right?'

'Everything's fine!' cried Pearl. 'Isn't it, Ben?'

'You surprise me,' Vic said soberly, pouring Chianti into
his soup. 'No goats? There were always goats in Arcady.'

'This is called Quattro Santo, signor.'

'Four saints, no less. Couldn't you get one good one?'

'They are all good.'

'And this place is four times blessed. Do you think some of it
will rub off? We certainly can do with a little blessing.'

'Scusi?'

'He means we're sinners,' said Pearl, 'all of us here, all of *us*,
he means. We don't know about you, do we, and anyway it's
none of our business.'

'He means we hope to benefit from our stay,' said Bennet
and Vic laughed and punched him on the shoulder.

The Harold Harpers and Wilma, coming in from the street,
said they had been round the piazza from which there was a
view of the Adriatic and that the trees, all the trees, were full
of electric light bulbs.

'What kind of soup's that?' said Wilma, looking into the
tureen.

'Tagliatelli in brodo, signora.'

Of course the girl might not know what it was all about but

she had to know what Vic's manner meant. Her face coloured darkly as she served Bennet and Pearl with soup. Pearl touched her hand.

'You mustn't mind, Gilda, we were only fooling.'

'That's right, Gilda,' said Vic. 'I'm an uncouth bastard.'

The girl hesitated, clasping the tureen in both arms she seemed about to turn and walk away. Then Vic leaned over and gently patted her hip. She smiled, the dark colour in her cheeks turned rosy and warm.

'Si, signor,' and she went to serve the Harpers, signalling with her bottom like a little white duck.

After that the dining-room filled with people from outside as well as the hotel guests and Cipriani, the proprietor, in flannel suit and grubby sneakers rolled from table to table asking was everyone happy.

Everyone was. There had been a change of heart like a change of wind and happiness went right through them. In fact Pearl felt that it went through the door and down the mountain for miles, though perhaps not as far as Rimini.

The meal was delicious, Pearl had second helpings. Gilda filled her plate and told her she must eat for two.

'I'm such a pig!'

Gilda smiled. 'A pig must eat for twenty.'

Vic picked the biggest golden peach out of Nell's hand and gave it to Pearl. 'That's for Higham.'

'Who?'

'All babies are Higham, born and unborn.'

Pearl's sense of belonging in this place was getting stronger, she couldn't remember having such a definite sense even back home.

'Not "back home", honey,' Ben corrected her, 'don't say "back home".'

'Well, I don't remember having it so much.'

'It's the Chianti. You're not used to it and you just drank up a whole glass.'

Pearl was sure that the looks she was getting from the big Italian women and the little Italian men weren't Chianti. She wasn't imagining, she was conditioned to indifference which was what one generally received and generally gave and she was as surprised as anyone that people she had never met and who didn't know her name should be nodding and smiling as if they knew *her* since before she was called Rubinsky or Patten or even Pearl.

'Will you look at that!' cried Wilma. 'They've switched on all the tuttifrutti lights.'

Everyone looked and cried out. In the square the trees signalled red, blue and orange as the breeze shook the light bulbs. And behind and above all the other colours was the luminous golden green of electrically lighted leaves.

'How lovely!' breathed Pearl.

'There will be dancing tonight,' said Cipriani. 'Tomorrow is the fiesta of Santa Lidia.'

'A fiesta! Oh, can we stay for it?'

'I think not. We're behind schedule and they're working overnight to fix the bus so that we can leave in the morning.'

Pearl asked Cipriani who Santa Lidia was.

'A good nice girl.'

'What was she sainted for?'

'For curing warts.'

Bennet said he had had an aunt who cured warts with fuse-wire but she was never canonised. Pearl pointed out that Lidia wouldn't have had the use of fuse-wire.

'We'll go dancing tonight, won't we? Under the trees?'

'Maybe.'

'Oh, Ben, it's the best thing we ever did, breaking down here!'

'Pearl, I want you to remember you're going to be a mother.'

Although she didn't say so, tonight Pearl intended to forget it. She already had. The past had brought her here and the future did not exist either for her or for the being inside her.

For him too, especially for him, there was only the present which she was living in and he was—not yet, not quite. He was still part of her, not invulnerable in that womb place because he had to be home when she was home, here when she was here, dancing when she danced.

While Ben wasn't looking she poured herself another glass of wine. 'Higham's going to dance,' she said, and drank. It tasted of wet iron and she grimaced approval.

They were setting off fireworks in the square. Probably there was too much light for the ground display to show up, but everyone enjoyed the noise.

'Do let's hurry and go out!' fretted Pearl.

'It sounds rough. Maybe you'd better stay inside.'

'Oh, Ben, please! There won't be another chance like this and you were glad of it you said. We should take this chance to break out of ourselves you said—'

'I did not say so, Pearl.' Bennet frowned as a great peppering of crackers ran across the square and finished, amid shrieks, under the hotel windows. 'If there's anything that bad in us we should try to change for the better, not run out on it.'

'I think so too,' said Pearl. 'But this is the first and last time I'll be here and every minute's important, I've got to really spend each minute. You brought me here, you brought *me*, not just Mrs. Bennet Rubinsky and the mother of your son.' Pearl laid all ten fingers on her breast. 'Remember me, Ben?'

She certainly didn't know herself, looking at him like that, and all she put into the look—she didn't suspect she had it in her. She caught the reflection in his eyes, there was a short sharp battle of Bennet Rubinsky which Pearl won and then felt sorry and reasonably guilty but unrepentant.

'All right, but not until we've had our coffee,' he said. 'It'll give them time to simmer down out there.'

Pearl thought they were more likely to boil over. She sat patiently while Bennet drank coffee and smoked a cigar. She was recalling how they had ground into Quattro Santo in bottom gear, the driver hanging on to the wheel. When the bus stopped in the square she had stayed in her seat while the others got out to stretch their legs. Their driver and guide went off to negotiate a night's stay at the hotel for the passengers while he took the bus into Forli for repair. She was tired, the roar of the engine had deafened her and Quattro Santo looked no different from any of the villages, hill or plain, that they had come through. It was perched among terraced fields and the same black cypresses and rusty chestnuts. It had white and yellow walls, crazy shutters and archways and pots of geranium and narrow streets with washing laced from house to house. She had been seeing Quattro Santo all day. It was as if a long-running movie had jammed and become a still.

Pearl did not much like the arriving on this trip. After hours of blundering at speed past brandished faces and places, when the bus finally stopped and set them down she felt she could get out of time the way she could get out of step. Well, it was feasible, with her it was feasible and she couldn't make much sense while part of her was still coming. She had been happy to stay in the bus for a while after they got to Quattro Santo.

Little by little, the place took on identity. The first thing she noticed when her ear-drums recovered from the battering, was that someone was practising on the church bell. An unusually light and silvery peal it was—perhaps because of the altitude— and very sweet and homey to listen to the ringer trying his carillon and never getting it quite right.

Then she noticed, on a twisted iron balcony no bigger than the fenders of their Plymouth saloon back home, an old brown woman tending a great lily with petals like the wattles of a cock. She was sponging its fat stem and its swollen leaves as if they were the body and hands of a sick child.

Then Pearl noticed how the stones in the road were worn, and the steps where people had put their feet going up and coming down to the same places for years. It shouldn't have engaged her, none of these trifling details should, because after all this was Europe and she was supposed to be absorbing only the best of it. But somehow they signified, very definitely.

She held Ben's hand across the table. 'I shall always remember tonight.'

'Pearl, if I refuse you anything it's for your own good.'

'I know.'

'And you'll let me be the judge?'

She was willing, had always been glad, in fact, for someone else to judge what was good for her. She couldn't herself have reached some of the conclusions, let alone acted on them. But if Ben was the judge tonight there would be only early bed and hot milk to remember, and a digest of the *Swiss Family Robinson* which they had started yesterday on the beach at Spezia. Could she really relish Papa Robinson's sturdy philosophising tonight?

She was spared any reply by Wilma Borg's coming to their table.

'Imagine, we're going to have a ball and all! Are you changing, Pearl?'

'Not my dress, but I'll put on some flatties so I can dance.' She got up, calling back to Ben, 'Do you know, Higham's looking forward to a dance,' and got away upstairs before he could say anything.

The girl Gilda was folding down the sheets in their room.

'Isn't it exciting?' cried Pearl. 'The fiesta and everything?'

Gilda smiled.

'To think we wouldn't be here if the bus hadn't broken down. We'd have gone right on to Rimini. We do keep going right on, you know. I didn't think about it before we came on this trip but it's so—encapsulating.'

'Signora?'

'You know, like space travellers. We should get down and make contact. That's what we're doing tonight.'

'Rimini is very fine. There are fine shops and hotels and beautiful villas. Here there is nothing.'

'Oh, you're wrong!'

'Here there is nothing,' Gilda repeated. It was a joy to watch her plump up the pillows and tighten the sheets. 'Here are still women who wash in the river with stones. Like this.' She seized up an ash-tray and beat the bedclothes with it.

Pearl sighed. 'I guess I like it for what it hasn't got as much as what it has. Don't do that, please!' The sky was an amalgam of blue and gold—platinum to the half-averted eye—the mountains were mauve, the villages sprinkled on them like crumbs. Pearl had not had time yet to look at it. 'Please don't close the shutters.'

'You like mosquitoes? These we have.' Gilda briskly slapped the shutters to. 'Of course if you like all night—' she bared her teeth and uttered a piercing whine from the back of her throat—'and this—' she slapped her own cheek and pretended to pick a dead insect out of her bosom.

'I guess not.'

Pearl sat down with her shoes in her hand. She liked the wheaten colour of the sheets—unbleached linen, she supposed—and they smelled like new bread. She wondered if they were laundered in the river.

'I was going as chambermaid in the Grand Hotel where are one hundred and fifty rooms,' said Gilda, laying out Pearl's nightdress. 'But my mother died and I stayed to keep house for my father and brothers.'

'What a shame.'

'Then I marry Nino, my third cousin.'

'Oh then it's not a shame.'

'Shame?' Gilda shook out Ben's pyjamas which he had rolled up and thrust into the overnight bag. She folded them and put them on the pillow next to Pearl's nightdress. 'Nino and me have been married three years.'

'So have we, almost. If my reckoning's correct our baby will come on our wedding anniversary.'

Gilda turned swiftly. 'Nino and me, we have no baby.'

'But you will—'

'We never have—I never have—' As she gazed at Pearl the colour rushed up her throat to the roots of her hair and was gone, leaving her strong white skin faintly glistening. 'Not once.'

'There's plenty of time!' cried Pearl. 'We didn't actually plan this for now. We were coming to Europe first and we were going to fix the house and we thought maybe after that we'd start a family. It happened right out of schedule. Ben says Nature breaks her own laws to achieve her ends.'

'My mother had three children when she had been married only two years.'

Pearl was going to say she must have made an early start, but thought better of it.

'I am a good Catholic, I ask the Virgin to give me a child, I make the pilgrimage. She hears other women, she hears cats, dogs, pigs!' cried Gilda. 'Me she makes barren!'

Pearl said firmly, 'Nonsense. You're the sort that has crowds of babies.'

Indeed she was, full-bosomed, wide-hipped, passionate dew on her skin, ripe, exactly ripe for procreation.

'Nino wants a son and I am barren!'

'Oh stuff! You're not at all. It might be his fault, your husband might be the one—you know what I mean?'

'Nino?' Gilda drew herself up with something like a smile but no fun in it. 'He is not the one!'

She was so vehement that Pearl blinked. 'Well, if there's any reason besides luck—good or bad, depends how you look at it—why you haven't conceived, it probably means you need a small operation, or hardly that—just some slight adjustment.'

'Adjustment?'

'Look, if you're worried you should see the doctor, have a check-up.'

'The dottore? He is good only like this—' Gilda pinched her own bottom and laughed, turning up her chin. Her bosom shook with laughter, her throat pulsed.

Pearl laughed too. She had a vision of a Restoration comedy scene, a skinny old man in rusty black chasing the rosy-cheeked maidservant.

They laughed until tears came and then Pearl wiped her cheeks. 'Gilda, you will have lots of sons.'

'I will have lots of sons, you will have lots of sons.'

'We'll have a baseball team! But tonight—' Pearl kicked off her shoes and they flew across the room—'tonight I'm going on the town.'

'Signora?'

'I'm going dancing in Quattro Santo in honour of your Saint—what's her name?—the one who cured warts?'

'Tomorrow is the day of Santa Lidia, the saint of little children.'

'Oh.' Pearl said softly, 'Shouldn't you pray to her?'

Gilda nodded. 'I light many candles. Nino too, he stops at the church on his way to work and lights a candle to Santa Lidia. He does not know I have seen him.'

'And I'll light a candle to her before we go! For you! She won't mind me not being Roman Catholic or anything, will she?'

Gilda shook her head, seeming not quite sure whether it was the done thing.

'It's not as if I'm an unbeliever,' said Pearl. 'I just happen to believe differently.'

When she bent to put on the flat shoes for dancing Gilda went on her knees and took the shoes from her. She gently drew on each one, smoothing Pearl's stockings over her ankles. 'Dolcemente, signora. You should be careful of yourself.'

'I should mix in. A pregnant woman is a power-house not a glass menagerie my paediatrician says.'

'Scusi?'

'He means we're tough, extraordinary tough, I guess. I will light a candle for you.' Gilda was still kneeling and Pearl couldn't resist touching her cheek. The flesh bloomed—that

74

was the word for it. What joy she must be, so many different joys. Pearl shyly lifted on her finger the strong blue-black ringlet in front of Gilda's ear. 'I'll pray to Santa Lidia to give you a baby.'

It seemed such a happy thought and might have helped in some way not apparent to themselves and anyhow it could do good, Pearl felt it could only do them both some good.

But Gilda moved her head aside. 'You are very kind, Signora,' and Pearl, who had been feeling wonderful, was confused by the way she said it.

Then Bennet came looking for her, asking was she ready, was she all right?

Gilda stood up in one swift movement and with lowered eyes went out of the room.

'What was that girl doing?'

'Putting on my shoes for me and I want to do something for her.'

'Like what?'

'Oh, I'm thinking,' Pearl said vaguely. It would only embarrass Ben, he spoke about the importance of getting outside himself but he wouldn't wish to get even a little way inside anyone else.

The band had arrived in the square and was setting up under the chestnut trees. There were half a dozen of them, middle-aged men in shirt sleeves and one, the tympanist, in waistcoat and no shirt. They had no music stands and no chairs. They stood or sat on the steps of the fountain. Only the saxophone player, a very fat man, wedged himself into an old basket chair and thereafter stood up and walked with the chair clamped to his hips. It seemed doubtful whether they would ever perform, they were so emotionally involved with artistic temperament or their own disharmony. So much arguing, shouting, pouting and shrugging surely could never put forth a concerted effort let alone a chord of music.

'We'll look around while they make up their minds,' said

Bennet and he and Pearl walked away from the coloured lights and through an arch into a street that tipped right down off the mountain.

'How ever do automobiles get up here?' said Pearl.

'They don't, this is for foot passengers only, on two feet or four.' Bennet pointed to a cigar-coloured donkey bringing up crates of canned beer.

'Ben, look—cobbles.' Pearl had to feel them with her fingers as well as the soles of her feet. 'They're warm, like just-laid eggs—aren't they like just-laid eggs?'

She began to see so much and wherever she looked was more, the eye couldn't get away for seeing.

'Come *on*, Pearl!'

'Ben, look—' She hadn't expected to see grass growing out of a street and just had to have it between her fingers to be convinced. 'Look how it's growing!'

'Pearl, will you please stand up!'

The houses leaned towards each other and scarcely beyond the heads of passers-by was the washing stirring in the breeze that came up, Ben said, warmed from the sea. Ben said the sea was like a griddle warming up the air all day.

The shops spilled out to their feet, so did the people, it was necessary to step over and round and wait for the women to move their chairs and the children to roll out of the way. What Pearl liked best was when the shutters weren't closed and she could see into the houses. Back home she wouldn't have thought of looking, she wouldn't have wanted to.

'How poor are these people?'

'By U.S. standards too poor to live.'

'The way they do live,' said Pearl, 'they've got style.'

'You shouldn't confuse it. There's more than one way of doing things and theirs is mostly the oldest way. That doesn't make it the most efficient.'

'I think so too.' Pearl was watching a woman buying live eels, running each one from her chin along the length of her arm.

'What you're calling style is what the Rubinskys left behind in Poland. It's how your great-grandfather made out in the Catskills and if they'd all stayed home you'd be bringing up the beer on a donkey.'

'We wouldn't have met. Did you think of that?' She tucked her hand into his armpit and they jolted over the cobbles and Pearl's full stomach rocked from her hip-joints.

Then they came to a clearing among the houses and in the middle was a church. Light streamed from the open door, the white-hot voltage of hundreds of devotional bulbs. They looked into a shell of pure glory. From the nave to the altar each grain of wood and stitch of fabric was glorified. Pearl felt slightly repelled and so probably did Bennet because he said, 'It's no place to bring your sins.'

Pearl wondered if Santa Lidia had a side chapel of her own, there was sure to be a statue and sconce. It would be only a gesture to light a candle in that blaze. Pearl was going to make it, but preferred not to in Ben's presence. His family had been Catholic and his recoil was total.

'It's clinical, I guess that's what they want from Confession.'

Bennet smiled. 'They won't confess tonight, they'll wait till after the fiesta.'

He led her away and Pearl made up her mind to come back first thing in the morning before he was awake. Perhaps there won't be so many lights on in the church, she thought, and my candle will show up.

An old woman in cinder-black passed them, surprising Pearl because her big feet were bare and the way they plunged in and out of her skirts seemed not directly to belong. It struck Pearl that the difference here would amount to much more than doing things one old way and she liked that, she liked the thought, she found it exciting. Yes, it was exciting to go on taking off layers, expecting and not caring that she could never get to the heart of it.

They came to a street of round arches with shops in them.

The shops were still doing business—fruit and meat and fish and an ice-cream parlour—but there was no getting away from the cold smell of stone. Three men sat round a marble slab playing cards. Stacked against the walls were new white tombstones and at the back of the shop a giantesque marble angel with wings outspread. How will they get it out? Pearl wondered. There were only these old vaulted doorways not much taller than a man's head.

The things to eat started her salivary glands working, she frankly coveted the sides of white salted pork, the strings of dark sausages, the butter in batons, the tubs full of olives. The bread too, sticky and spiced, and trays of rich bright things too small for cookies and too big for candies—she'd have taken them all if they'd have travelled and never mind the bibelots.

Bennet bought some of the cookie things packed in a cone of thin brown biscuit. They ate them right away, walking under the arches, it was the first time Pearl had eaten the wrapper as well.

She hadn't seen so many birds in cages before either, packed in, wing to wing.

'Why, they're wild birds,' she said distastefully and put her finger on the bars and at once every one of the wretched little prisoners panicked and tried to fly. There was such a whirring and struggling and beating of wings in the tiny space that she snatched her hand behind her back with a cry.

It was over in a moment, they fell on each other panting and dishevelled, a heap of tiny brown and black feathered birds with gaping beaks and legs no thicker than pins.

'They're wild birds!' Pearl said again, this time with dismay. The shopkeeper came out all smiles and tapped the cage, but the birds were too exhausted to do more than flutter feebly. 'Isn't there any law about that?'

Bennet shook his head. 'The wonder is that there are any left to catch by now.'

'But it's awful!' The shopkeeper was talking earnestly to

Pearl, winking and nodding and several times he plucked at his shoulders as if he were pulling off wings. She shuddered. 'Whatever is he saying?'

'I think he's telling you they're good to eat.'

'To *eat!*'

'That's so. They roast them on sticks, sort of a kebab.'

'Oh no!'

Pearl's revulsion was obvious even to the shopkeeper. He turned away, shrugging and spreading his hands, palms up.

'I guess it's some more of their style,' Bennet said, smiling.

'It's awful, and it's not as if they haven't plenty else to eat.' Pearl pointed to the cage and asked the man, 'How much do you want for them?'

'Signora?'

'How much? Quanto costa?'

'Pearl!'

'Tre cento cinquanta lire.'

'Three hundred and fifty? Ben, that's only a dollar for the lot!'

The Italian held up one finger. 'Una, una, signora.'

'He means each. Pearl, you're crazy if you're thinking what I think you are.'

'Ask him how much for all of them. Tutto!' cried Pearl to the shopkeeper. Whereupon he began to do sums on his fingers.

'Pearl, it's madness. What are you going to do with them?'

'What do you think? I'm going to set them free.'

'Cinque mille lire,' said the shopkeeper.

'Pearl, he's having you on. I'm not paying twenty dollars for a cage of birds!'

'Ben, please!'

'No!'

The shopkeeper, watching their faces, smiled knowingly. He put his hand into the cage, took out a bird, dropped it into a paper bag and gave the bag to Pearl.

'Signora, prego!'

'But I want them all!'

Ben took her arm. 'Pearl, he's giving you the darn thing. Stop arguing and come away.'

'Giving it to me?' Pearl looked at the smiling man. 'It's not his to give, it's a free creature.'

'Prego, signora!'

'Look, Pearl, if you bought the cage full and set them all free you know what would happen? They'd be caught again tomorrow.'

'But how?'

'I don't know. With bird lime and snares.' Bennet said bitterly, 'What chance do they have?'

Pearl sighed. 'I suppose I'm a phoney wanting to buy sausages and wild birds.'

'What?'

'Never mind, let's get away from here.'

As they went, Pearl gingerly carrying the paper bag, the shopkeeper laughed and made fluttering gestures with his hands.

'That man's a brute.'

'He's no St. Francis,' said Bennet. 'Who is?'

They went to the end of the street and found a courtyard with an acacia-tree and one side open to the scrubby start of an olive-grove.

'It's quiet here,' said Pearl, 'and the bird can fly up into the tree.' She opened the bag. Nothing happened, the bird did not move. 'Why doesn't it fly out?'

'It can't. Also it's scared.' Ben took the bag, took the bird in his hand and threw it into the air. It fell to the ground, not like a stone so much as a leaf drifting and Pearl exclaimed in dismay. Then it opened its wings, sprang up and was gone.

Pearl laughed. 'That one won't get caught again, it's a wise bird now.' She was relievedly, enormously happy. 'Wasn't it nice of that man to give it to me?'

'You're crazy like a fox, Mrs. Rubinsky, and I love you.'
Bennet kissed her and they walked with their arms round each
other as they used before they were married—and after, though
not very lately because Pearl was sensitive about putting her
big stomach in front of Bennet.

They found their way back to the hotel by following the
direction of general noise pent up in the piazza. It was hard
to believe that the place had been quiet when they saw it first.
Bennet estimated there was about a thousand people there,
counting those on the balconies and roofs and leaning out of
windows, all noisy in themselves or in their musical instru-
ments or anything they could bang or blow or twang on. And
they were all in motion round the piazza like the stuff breaking
and rising, flashing and rolling in a fast-boiling pot.

'My, what a scrimbash,' said Bennet.

'Look, Vic and Nell and the Harold Harpers are over there.
Let's go to them.'

Pearl plunged into the crowd. Bennet, protesting, followed.
It was quite a battle getting to Vic Farrar and the Harpers.
Vic saw them and came to help Pearl.

'Isn't it fun?' cried Pearl.

'It's Walpurgis night,' said Vic.

The staid Nell was dancing with herself, her arms clasped
about her shoulders. A boy perched in a tree played his
accordion for her alone.

'Pearl, take care!' cried Bennet, temporarily penned behind
a string of girls who had joined hands.

'Take care of Higham,' said Vic.

'Higham wants to dance.' Pearl too clasped her arms around
herself—across her stomach not her chest—and waltzed to Nell's
music. She felt wonderful, light as air and warm as wine and
roses. The boy smiled at her as he played and the breeze rocked
the silly bare light bulbs in the chestnut tree.

Then there was no more dancing, they were pushed back
against the buildings to accommodate a procession coming into

the square. A phalanx of children led, boys in rough white robes and girls in dusty black carrying long peeled sticks with which they struck out, not too much in fun, at people as they passed.

After the children came an old man staggering under a heavy embroidered banner, then a company of nuns followed by boys carrying cardboard lions on sticks and a papiermâché dragon draped over the heads and shoulders of two men on bicycles and riskily lit by candles from inside.

The tail of the dragon clowned around, catching up with its head, riding beside it, pedalling madly past or darting from side to side honking an absurdly falsetto hooter. It was miraculous how he avoided crashing or setting himself alight. The crowd roared slavishly at his every antic. The trumpets and drums of the band following him in blue and silver uniforms were drowned in shouts of 'Bigallo!'

Finally, on a kind of silver cake-round carried by two men came a big plaster figure. It had just been repainted, the colours were bright and sticky, red where red ought to be – white, blue, green, yellow, scrupulously laid on – the map of a girl. Vic said it was Lidia, one of the four patron saints of the town.

'Reminds me of a Chev I had once, I put so many skins of paint on her she was wholly sealed up, you couldn't open the doors or lift the nose or turn the wheels for paint.'

Pearl felt sorry for Lidia. The bearers tilted her so that her chaplet of flowers slid down to her nose. She wasn't getting any reverence. In point of fact, Pearl was thinking, the tone was altogether temporal. Everywhere she looked was this down-to-earthness: the ancient was ancient with years and use and still was being used; the beautiful was something else first – a lot of other things first – and beautiful in the last resort. And so holiness, if there was any, would have to be earned and not just seen. Presumably Lidia earned hers sometime.

The dragon was bringing the tone down further, or its tail was. Its tail certainly was. One of the wheels of the rear bicycle became wedged and amid shouts and laughter the rider fell off. Everyone shouted 'Bigallo!' but the procession moved on without him, the dragon steadily cycling and pulling its empty tail.

Of course he had fixed to fall off so that everyone should see him. He was everyone's fool tonight, a wedge-shaped man with a big head and shoulders tapering to a pair of legs bowed like a baby's. He wore only a waistcoat and shorts and a string of cobnuts round his neck and was either very swarthy or very hairy—he didn't stay still long enough for Pearl to get a good look at his face. The act was to try to mount the bicycle, and as unrehearsed slapstick it was pretty good. His ferocity undermined every move, he employed enormous guile which recoiled on himself; the bicycle defeated him simply and calculably by falling the way he did not expect it to fall, or refusing to go forward with him when he was already launched and in motion.

Round and round he chased, snatching, tripping, piling up with his face in the spokes and his baby-doll legs kicking and the crowd jeered and laughed and stamped and egged him on. If he did manage to mount the machine and began to wobble away someone would reach out and hold the back wheel until he lost his balance and keeled over on his back, the bicycle on top and his feet still furiously pushing at the pedals.

Finally he lost his temper, or pretended to, and tearing off his necklace of cobnuts threw them at the crowd. Women retaliated with flowers which dropped at his feet and then boys aimed olives at him. He pantomimed fury, shadow-boxed the crowd and charged it and fell flat in the best custard and whitewash tradition.

'We could use him to warm up our ball games,' said Vic.

Pearl had never liked clowning, she worried about the mess. Her instinct was to cover up for anyone making a fool of himself, she was sorry for this man. He was filthy from rolling on the ground and his chest and shoulders were scraped raw.

She wondered at the work he put into it, the unkindness to himself. Wasn't there a greed about the way people shouted and gestured – as if they couldn't get enough? Was it worth being popular so? Wasn't it too close to being *un*popular?

Suddenly Bigallo picked up his bicycle and rode away. He had either had enough or he wanted to catch the procession. Then the crowd began to move, the bulk-up broke into private eddies. People began to laugh their own laughter and call to each other. But while there was still space around Pearl and Bennet and Vic and Nell and the Harold Harpers, the throwing started.

Vic was the first to be hit. It was nothing worse than an applecore and he grimaced and smiled as he brushed it away. Then Harold uttered an exclamation and put his hand to his face.

'Who threw that?'

Who indeed? People were strolling, talking, singing, some were dancing with their arms across each other's necks. Urchins they suspected but those in sight were scuffling among themselves on the ground.

Then Bennet was struck on the chest. He picked up a small hard olive and even as he straightened he received another full in the face. At the same moment Nell, who was twirling again to the music of the boy in the tree, looked mildly round, rubbing the back of her neck.

'It's from over there,' said Vic. 'Behind the fountain.'

Pearl had already seen. Among so much movement, a group of faces steadily turned were as alerting almost as a streamer. And she was aware of something outcoming across the crowds to them. They were all at the receiving end – Ben and Vic and Nell and the Harpers – why did she feel that she was the focal point? Did she feel that?

'Isn't that the girl from the hotel?' said Vic.

They were all young people and probably it was the holiday, the occasion more than anything they had drunk which had put them in such spirit. Probably they could do as much for each other as the rusty red wine of the hillside and what they did was probably harmless and the germ of harm was slipped them halfway. They were laughing and aiming at the Americans with rubbish from the basin of the fountain, mostly rotten fruit and balled-up cartons, wet and unpleasant but not dangerous. Gilda, the hotel-maid, was with them. Or they were with her. They encouraged each other with their throws and with their hits, but the source was this girl, white-skinned, black-haired, hanging on the arm of a heavy-browed young man—her husband, probably. She was excited, her cheeks flaming, her full lips laughing, crying out or pressed to her wrist in delight.

'Goddamit,' said Vic, ducking to avoid a soggy orange rind, 'what started this?'

'Why don't we do something?' cried Mrs. Harold Harper.

'It's only in fun,' said Pearl, 'we should try to understand that.'

She was thinking that it might take a little more time than they had. Not that people here were so complicated or so different, just that she had other expectations, so did Vic and the Harold Harpers, everyone did. And Bennet, of course, knew what she meant—he had meant it first, anyway.

'Pearl's got something. We shouldn't try to apply our standards.'

Vic picked wet pith off his lapel. 'I don't know if I can go along with some of theirs.'

'You don't have to. Just suspend judgment and take back collateral impressions.'

Pearl saw Gilda quite clearly. Gilda was laughing, she looked like those ripe glowing girls the old masters loved to paint. The sulky-browed young man stooped towards her, his hand possessively on her neck. Gilda turned and looked directly at Pearl. She raised her arm, Pearl was just about to wave back when something struck her full on the forehead.

The blow was as sudden as a clap of darkness. Involuntarily she must have shut her eyes. She opened them and everything was pouring with light—red, green, gold, even Bennet was ablaze. She cried out, held out her hands, she couldn't see who took them and she was terribly afraid of falling and pulling that person down with her.

'Pearl!'

'She's been hit!'

'She's bleeding!'

'No,' Pearl said sharply. 'It's not blood, it's the lights, something happened to the lights.'

Bennet was looking at his palm. 'Here's what they threw. A stone—they threw a stone at her!'

'Nell, help me get her into the hotel.'

'I'm going to find who threw this and give him the hiding of his life!'

'Leave it!'

'Leave it? Till when? Till they make a killing? I'm going to beat hell out of them!'

'Someone should do that!' cried Mrs. Harold Harper.

'Don't be a fool.' Vic seized Ben by the back of his jacket. With one twist he had the jacket off Ben's shoulders and pinioned his arms in it. 'Do you want to start a riot?'

'I'm not scared of those hoodlums—' Wrenching and squirming, Bennet fought Vic's hold. He dropped to his knees to try to break it. 'Damn you! Let go!' Vic was stronger than Bennet and all Bennet could seem to break was the buttons off his shirt.

'I'm not thinking only of that bunch,' said Vic. 'The whole town's lit up and God-happy and ready for anything, including mayhem.' He shoved Bennet before him towards the hotel. 'Nell and Mrs. Harper, please bring Pearl and let's get the hell out of this.'

And Pearl was frogmarched away too as if she was tending to be troublesome, she who had never felt less like troubling anyone. She just wanted to be in some dark place years from now, with a cold coin on the middle of her forehead. There was a burning hot one there, she was going to have a long, long headache.

And she was upset about what was being done to Bennet. He fought Vic every inch to the hotel, with people laughing and calling heaven knew what at him. They thought he was drunk.

When they reached the lobby he stopped struggling and went quiet and stiff. Vic held his arms and his shirt collar gapped and he looked ready to burst into tears. Cipriani came forward with cries of concern as well he might: they hadn't made much of a carnival night re-entry.

Nell and Mrs. Harold took Pearl upstairs and made her lie on her bed. They bathed her forehead: the skin was broken, Nell said, but not to worry. Mrs. Harold said she didn't understand anything and wished someone would explain. Pearl wished the same, but who was qualified to do it?

Bennet came and took her hand. 'Pearl, is it bad? Does it hurt?' He gripped and shook her fingers, he was primarily very angry. Anger was a primary feeling and came before love, thought Pearl, way before love.

'No, it isn't bad. I was just surprised I guess.' And surprised for a longer time than that minute. 'It's stopped hurting.'

'Why should they *start* to hurt you? You of all people!'

'I'm not special,' said Pearl.

'You wouldn't hurt a soul!' Bennet indignantly crumpled her hand and then sandwiched it gently between his. 'Pearl, are you going to be O.K.?'

'She's going to have a headache,' said Mrs. Harold.

'We should get a doctor to check her over—'

'In this place?' said Mrs. Harold. 'What kind of doctor do you expect to get here? Let her rest and take a little aspirin if she must. I had it through pregnancy without ill effect, but strength of mind is the only recommendation I really care to give.'

Mrs. Harold and Nell left soon after and Bennet went at once to the window.

'That bunch is still down there fooling about among themselves. I don't see the girl.'

'What girl?'

'From the hotel. She was with them.'

'She wasn't.' Pearl shut her eyes. It wasn't true, either, that the bruise had stopped hurting. In the middle of her forehead she felt every contour of the stone that had hit her. 'They were strangers, all of them, and they were only fooling.'

'The blood on your face wasn't fooling.' Bennet soberly buttoned his shirt. 'I was ready to take them all on. I could have, Pearl.'

'I know.'

'Vic Farrar said that's what they wanted, to provoke us. I didn't care if they did or not, it was what *I* wanted.'

Against her eyelids Pearl could see the bruise. It was X-shaped, a cross of purple fire. 'I'm glad you let them go.'

'Vic stopped me. He had a jackhold, but if I could have broken it I'd have gone for them. I'd have broken Vic's arms, Pearl, and gone for them.'

'I'm glad you didn't fight. I think I'd have died.'

'A man has his feelings.'

'I know.' She said softly, 'I know about your feelings.'

'He was right though, Vic was right to stop me. Why, it was nearly an international incident.'

Pearl raised herself on her elbow and reached towards the dressing-table. She was going to look in the hand-mirror at the mark on her forehead. 'You mean there could have been a war about it?'

'Now did I say that? Did I mention a nuclear holocaust? You're putting words in my mouth again, Pearl. It could get us in serious trouble. This isn't America, this is Europe and they're jumpy as hell.'

It brought tears to her eyes and a lump to her throat. 'I wish we were home!'

'Look at it this way. We're ambassadors here, I'm not putting it too high to say that. What these people think of us is what they're going to think of America. Vic could see that, he thought for all of us. It isn't everyone can do that, Pearl, at a time like that.'

'Nell wasn't hurt.'

'I just wonder if I'd have had the foresight to hold *him* back if she had been. We can only hope so.' Ben looked at her soberly. 'It's not so much of a bruise.'

It was more of a graze really, where the sharp edge of the stone had broken the skin the threads of blood had dried already. There was no point in saying that it had broken much more, that she had the sensation of a great star-shaped fissure. In what? The window of my soul, she thought. Oh my!

'No, it's really nothing.'

'Are you sure you feel — In yourself — ' Ben gingerly touched the blanket over her stomach — 'in the essential, I mean, you feel secure?'

'I feel fine.'

'Rest is what you need. Rest and quiet.' He closed the windows on the sound of music from the piazza. They were dancing now, crammed together, back to back. Pearl wondered if Nell's little soloist had found someone else to play to. 'I think I'll go and talk to Vic. Will you be O.K., honey?'

'I'll be fine.'

'I'll be right back.'

He went out, gently closing the door. He was going to talk to Vic, acknowledge Vic's responsibility, give him best. Bennet was ready — anxious, in fact — to do that when he believed it was due and he was going to think a lot of Vic Farrar from now on. Vic had just got himself that distinction.

Pearl put down the hand-mirror and lay back on the pillows. She started to relax the way she had been taught, toes first — tightening and letting go, ankles, calves, knees, thighs, right through her body to her scalp. Her scalp was where she should have finished, but she could neither tighten nor slacken her forehead. She had no muscles left in her forehead.

'It's localised anyway.' She patted her stomach. 'You're all right, Higham.'

She wouldn't be getting up early tomorrow to light a candle. She didn't wish anything for the girl, good or bad. She was sorry for her, but that was only a quarter of the story because besides Gilda and her need was Gilda's husband and his need. And besides sorrow which Pearl had now, there was splendour which she had had for seven months. This evening, right up until the almost international incident, she had felt very, very splendid. Perhaps it was the splendour that the stone had broken.

Had she been responsible, like Vic, thinking of other people and not just of herself, she would get up tomorrow early and light two candles for Gilda. Gilda certainly could use them. I would, thought Pearl, if I believed they'd do any good, if I thought they'd really do something for her – it did not seem illogical to insist on that now, whereas before the gesture had been nice enough and the thought sufficient – but of course it's nonsense. I wouldn't be justified in contributing, morally I'd be wrong, playing at responsibility. I should ask her point-blank why she threw a stone at me, make her say why so that she understands it herself.

Was that what she should do? But she wasn't like Vic and she didn't have to study to be like him. She rolled over, but nowadays it was pretty uncomfortable lying on her side. Groaning, she rolled back and found herself looking up into Gilda's face.

It was a physical shock and Pearl's body reacted at once. It bore down on the bed, absurdly trying to shrink its stomach, and she had a half-second to observe this. Of course she had known that she would almost certainly have to face Gilda again and she had accepted it that way. She didn't think – she didn't even think it would be more fitting to think – that Gilda would almost certainly have to face her.

She must have cried out with alarm because Gilda said, 'Signora?', inclining her head on her strong white neck.

Pearl pushed herself up on her elbows. She had not expected the facing to be like this, with her stretched out, disadvantaged, on her bed. She would have slipped off and got to her feet, but Gilda put a hand on the bed on either side and leaned over Pearl.

'Are you not well, Signora?'

Pearl's heart beat uncomfortably. She was sweating, which she practically never did, and quite independently her right arm went across her stomach which she had been taught never to try to hide but to carry in pride and joy. She was scared, her instinct was not to trust this girl and a purely animal instinct it was—nothing to do with reason. Reason urged Pearl to challenge the girl, make her think what she had done, why she had done it.

'I have a headache.'

What was it that Pearl instinctively feared, apart from the capacity to throw stones? Of course Pearl would never have that capacity herself, she wouldn't want to do anyone that kind of harm. But of course that wasn't the harm Gilda wanted to do Pearl, not stone-throwing, not really.

'A headache?'

She was a beautiful girl: presently she would coarsen and fatten and this she would let happen and in her heavy white body would be the same fear and rage. But she was beautiful now and the fear and rage could be forgiven.

'Gilda—' Pearl said softly, but Gilda cried, 'A headache?' and leaned over and ungently touched the centre of Pearl's forehead. When Pearl flinched and tried to turn her head away she laughed.

'Why do you want to hurt me?'

'Hurt?' Gilda's throat arched and her tongue curled back between her teeth with laughter. 'Here we lie down for a man, not a headache!' She ran to the window and with a thrust of her arms burst the shutters apart. 'You should dance. All night. We shall all dance all night, every man with every girl until the feet bleed!'

Pearl shuddered. The noise of the band came brassing over the noise of the crowd, her head throbbed to a strict tempo, the lights jazzed in her eyes.

'Please shut the window.'

'You are not sick! Women have babies all the time.'

'Yes,' said Pearl, 'don't they?' and they gazed at each other, Gilda with her back to the window and the fleering lights, Pearl on the bed, propped on her hands behind her spreading stomach. It wasn't international, it was their own incident.

Gilda suddenly came back to the bed and dropped to her knees. Pearl cried out in alarm as she pulled away the blanket.

'What are you doing?'

Gilda put her ear to Pearl's stomach. 'I am listening to the life.'

Fixing Pixie Loveless

LUMLEY was fretting about the girl. She was on his mind, she was on all their minds, but Lumley fretted. Fish asked if he was scared of her. 'Scared of a little kid — six, seven years old — are you?'

'I'm a thinking man, Goldy, which you're not. Thinking requires something up top besides hair.'

Fish shook his yellow curls out of his collar. 'Then tell us what you thought when you thought of bringing her here.'

'I thought she'd hang the job on us.'

'She can't hang anything on me, I've never been in trouble.'

'Trouble?' Lumley went into a bronchial paroxysm of laughter.

Fish couldn't bear the crackling and curdling of Lumley's chest. It revolted him. He screamed at Lumley and stamped his foot. Lumley was expiring with laughter but they both stopped immediately Ritter told them to.

'I'll finish the two of you, so help me God!' But Ritter, they knew, wouldn't need God's help.

Lumley had stuffed the inside pockets of his coat with money, such a wad of banknotes that the coat stood off from his chest. 'I put my hand over her mouth and then what could I do? She had her breath all drawn up ready to yell.'

They wouldn't forget. They had each been working, each doing his part, with just a chip of time to do it in, knowing they couldn't depend on a minute more or be sure that they wouldn't have to manage with a minute less. And it was going well they felt in their bones, not needing even to nod to each other. They worked as one, solidly and sensitively, and as one they looked up and saw the girl. Their three skins crept, it was the last of their solidarity.

She had been in the manager's office all the while, curled up on a shelf — what a place to be, between acid-flasks and an old foam fire-extinguisher! — she had a blanket and pillow and was watching them, chin in hand. Who had put a dark-faced kid halfway up the wall?

They had seen her actually decide to cry out. As if she had been waiting to get their attention first she pushed herself into a sitting position, filled her chest and opened her mouth. It was like watching a juke box go into operation after putting sixpence in.

'There was no time to gag her.'

The job was finished, they were on their way and the guard was on his, checking every door as he came along the passage. Lumley had done the only possible thing in the circumstances.

'We couldn't know he had his kid with him. It's against the security rules. He's going to have to own up. When they find the money's gone he'll have to tell them the girl's gone too. I wouldn't like to be in his shoes.'

They could afford to smile. The job couldn't have been better done if they had been professionals. They went into the place and did what they had to do and each thing latched on to another so neatly that they had felt — feeling as one — that it was history already.

Then Lumley said, 'We'll have to fix the kid.'

'Fix her?'

'Or she'll talk. She's had a good look and she'll know us again.'

'How do you fix a kid?'

'How do you fix anyone?'

Fish had already made up his mind about Lumley. He didn't need to ponder Lumley's motives, they were all of the same colour and there was no need to keep on being shocked. But

Fish was shocked just the same, he had not learned to conserve his emotion.

'Get yourself life if you like,' said Ritter, 'but not while you're working for me.'

Lumley's ears went back. He tapped the money in his chest pocket—the first thing it had bought him was nerve—'I'm working for Edgar Lumley and no kid's going to put me inside.'

Ritter went to the window. The other two, jumpy, had been constantly moving about, pacing to and fro, brushing round the four walls like flies, but this was the first time that Ritter had left his seat. Alerted, they watched him. On this moonless night, with nothing familiar for even their minds' eyes to place, they were willing, and eager, to believe that he could see farther than they could. Ritter had arranged everything, told them where the money was and how much, and what they must perform to get it. They had performed as he had said and they had the money as he had said. They waited now for what else he would say.

'We'll leave her.'

'Leave her! To talk?'

'She can't talk about us.'

'She can't? She can't tell them it was Bill Ritter, Edgar Lumley and a strawberry blond called Fish that blew B. J. Riley's safe on Thursday night?'

'She doesn't know us from Adam and there's nothing to connect us,' Ritter said patiently. 'The only danger is that if she talks right away she could put them on our tail. So we'll leave her where she won't be found right away.'

'At the bottom of a well?'

'It'll be light in a couple of hours so that's how much time we've got.' Ritter turned from the window. 'Get the car, Edgar.'

Lumley went out to the shed. He tramped through the snarled grass that had grown unchecked all summer, the money in his pockets pressed like two loving hands on each breast. He had never done a job of this importance before and was feeling inspired. He foresaw a bright future, against the slabs of dark it was very bright and very private.

The shed was padlocked, a precaution they had taken although this girl couldn't walk out. 'Someone could walk *in*,' Ritter had said, 'like a tramp looking for a place to sleep.' He believed in taking care of eventualities. Lumley was for cutting them off short. He shone his torch into the back of the car.

They all knew that the girl couldn't walk, her crutches had lain beside her on the shelf and had been left there, but Lumley's stomach turned over when he saw nothing on the back seat, only the blanket they had wrapped her in. He snatched open the car door and the blanket heaved and she looked out from under it. She did not blink, her eyes were two guns aimed at his head.

He hastily switched off the torch. 'What are you doing?'

She didn't care for the dark she said, and wrestled with the blanket, tutting her annoyance. 'It comes so *close*!'

The blanket or the dark, Lumley didn't care which—he got into the car and slammed the door. He had reasons for backing out without lights: so as not to risk attracting attention from the road, and so as not to let her get another look at his face.

'I cried and cried. Didn't you hear me?'

'Crying? You should be ashamed of yourself.'

Lumley had lifted her down from the shelf and carried her, dodging cylinders and trolleys and things that he needed both hands to advise him of in the semi-gloom. She was what he had carried out of that place—his prize! Lucky for him that Ritter and Fish were there to bring the money, lucky for them that he was there to bring the girl.

'Are we going home?'

He asked would she like to be and she said scornfully that

he must be joking. Damned kids, he thought, they're not grateful to their parents.

'Are we going somewhere nice?'

Lumley had found her surprisingly heavy. She was as solid as a cricket ball but her legs dangled as he ran and her heels had struck his shins. Carrying her was painful.

He enquired, 'What's wrong with your legs?'

'They're paralysed. Where are the other men? Where's the one with the pretty hair?'

'Shut up.'

'Why did you bring me here if you don't like me?'

'To keep you quiet.'

'I wasn't going to make a noise.'

'You opened your mouth like a church door. We saw you.'

'I wouldn't have screamed. Sometimes I breathe in and out my mouth to stop my back aching.' She leaned on the seat behind him and blew into his ear. 'Like this. It lets the pain out.'

He was reversing out of the shed at that moment and would have struck her if he'd had a free hand, perhaps it would have done them all some good.

'You'll be sure to tell them what you saw, won't you? Every little detail? Don't you forget any,' he said viciously. 'Details are important.'

'I don't always tell people what they want to know.'

'Suppose we made it worth your while to keep your mouth shut?' Lumley wheezed with laughter. 'What's your price?'

'Why does your chest make that noise?'

'Would a fiver satisfy you?'

'I don't want money, I've got bags of money, all the money in the world.'

Lumley's face stiffened, his chest roared and crackled, but not with laughter. The noise of his chest was harsher than the steady purr of the engine.

He had to switch the headlights on to see where he was in relation to the yard gate. He also saw the first rain for days slanting on the dark. That's all we need, he thought, tyre and foot-marks for them to get their callipers on.

'If you promise to take me for a ride every day I won't tell. I do so like riding in cars.'

'I wouldn't give you car room.' Lumley fell out and slammed the door and shouted 'Rag legs!' through the window.

Ritter jumped on him as soon as he got into the house. 'Dead quiet I said! What are you trying to do? Advertise us?'

'Cars have engines, bits of metal making crap, crap, crap—a car won't go dead quiet.'

'I'm not talking about the car, I'm talking about you.'

'The thinking man,' supplied Fish.

'That girl's got no morals. She tried to get me to bribe her. Me!' cried Lumley. 'If we don't fix her she'll tell everything she knows and a lot more that she doesn't. She's got to be fixed before she fixes us.'

'Or before you do.'

Lumley kicked Fish's bottom and Fish lashed out with his kitten-stroke at Lumley's jaw. Ritter went between them and with a chop of his hand knocked up first Lumley's and then Fish's long bony nose. Fish cried out with shock and pain.

'Now listen. You're going to take that girl where she won't be found. You're going to run the car into the woods, right in under the trees and lock it and leave it.'

'Who's going to?' cried Lumley. 'Who are you looking at?'

'One of us. We'll draw for it.' Ritter took out a wad of banknotes and snapped off the elastic that held them. 'The lowest number gets the job.'

'We're all in this, we all stand to lose if she talks.'

'There's no point in multiplying the risk. Take a note.'

Lumley grumbled but he took a note, so did Fish, then Ritter. Fish drew the low number.

'The girl will be pleased.' Lumley grinned. 'She fancies you, Goldfish.'

Ritter held out his hand as Lumley was about to pocket the

note he had drawn and told Fish, 'Three miles from here, a mile the other side of Hy Cross, a track runs off the road. Follow it till it forks. Take the right and run in under the trees as far as you can. There's a bank and a sharpish slope into an old clay pit. Get out of the car, take the handbrake off and let her roll. She'll settle at the bottom out of sight.'

'How long for?'

'Long enough.'

'And the girl?'

Ritter had red pockets under his eyeballs and sometimes looked like a spaniel. 'The girl can't walk.'

'I shouldn't have to do it, Lumley should. He brought her, let him do it!'

'Get clear as fast as you can and don't thumb a ride afterwards, walk across country to the Junction and take a train home.'

'I've left home. I'm going away.'

'Where to?'

'That's my business.'

'I must know, Derek,' said Ritter, 'for all our sakes. I may need to get in touch.'

'Some touch. I'll be in Vietnam.'

'Vietnam!' Lumley's voice cracked. 'What the bloody hell for?'

'To help the bloody children!'

There was a silence which Fish endured, stiff in every hair with rage. The idea leaked into the corners of the room, then Ritter sighed, unregretfully blew out his lips.

'You'll have to go home, Derek.'

'I'll do as I like.'

'You'll have to go home just as if it was any other day and you'll stay there until you hear from me.'

'Home?' cried Fish. 'What's the good of the money at home?'

Lumley picked the strap of Fish's rucksack off his shoulder. 'You won't have the money if you don't co-operate.'

99

He had seen Fish stow his share away in the rucksack. Fish had climbed a fifteen-foot gate and crept on finger and toe-tips along a narrow ledge. They couldn't have got inside the factory without him but as all he had done was climb they gave him the smallest cut. He had told them, 'I'm the one that risked his neck', but they wouldn't allow him a penny more and they watched him like uncles while he put his share away.

He tried to pull the strap of his rucksack out of Lumley's grip but he merely pulled it off his back and he and Lumley were left holding a strap each.

'Let go!'

'You don't get paid till you've finished the job.'

'I have finished it!'

'Not till you fix the girl.'

'You'll get your money back later,' said Ritter and took the rucksack from them. 'We're in your hands, Derek.'

Fish didn't feel his age, he had that uncles feeling about Ritter and Lumley and he felt like a child.

'Give me that rucksack or I'll—I'll—' What could he do against wicked uncles? His rage was a head of steam which had been getting up all his life. The world was full of Ritter and Lumley and hope was the reason they succeeded, silly bloody hope that people just couldn't be like that. 'I could fix *you*—I only have to say one word, I'd get off with probation but they'd put you away for years.'

'The money's yours and you'll get it when you've fixed the girl.' Ritter hung the rucksack over his shoulder. 'You have my word.'

'What more do you want?' Lumley winked.

Fish's rucksack hung like a hump under Ritter's neck and all Fish could say was, 'My pyjamas are in there.'

'You've got his word, you won't need money if you've got that.' Lumley's chest rustled with laughter. 'And you won't need pyjamas, men don't wear pyjamas—'

'I don't give tuppence for a dictionary of his damned words!'
Fish could have wept but wouldn't, he would never forgive
his tear ducts if they operated in front of Ritter and Lumley.
He made the worst gesture he knew, twice—once in each of
their faces—and flung the door back on its hinges. Ritter, who
insisted on caution, sprang after him, but Fish ran out willing
someone to see the light and come to investigate. 'Please
God, please Jesus, make them get caught—*now* if there's any
justice—or be a Fraud for ever and ever, amen.'

The darkness was thick enough to taste and it tasted like
mud. What had he done to deserve this? He had sweated
along a two-inch parapet above a fifty-foot drop into a cast-
iron vat: gashed himself on barbed wire, jumped when he was
told to jump. Justice shouldn't be for him only, if he tasted
mud those two should eat dirt. Now that he could weep in
private his tears remained unshed. Who could he trust—with
Ritter and Lumley at one end and the Holy Damned Fraud
at the other? He walked into the side of the car and collected
a cut lip.

The girl had managed to climb into the front passenger seat.
She was supposed to be completely immobile—at least Ritter
and Lumley supposed so and now Fish liked the thought of
their being wrong, it could be the beginning of justice for
them. He could of course have walked away and left them to
it. And to his share of the money. It would be a miracle if he
ever got that. He licked his burst lip. 'Work a miracle, you
Holy Damned Fraud!'

As he slid into the driver's seat the girl said, 'It's you. I'm
glad. I like you. I like your hair, I can just see it. My father says
only bad boys have long hair.'

Fish would have liked her to be dumb as well as lame. She
was his very bad luck, fate could hardly have organised worse
for him. He started the engine and revved it to a scream, he
also switched on the headlamps and punched the horn as he
roared out of the gate.

'Where are we going? I'm glad those men aren't coming, it'll be lovely on our own. It's a lovely car. Make it go fast. You can't go too fast for me.'

Fish had done no wrong until now. Climbing a gate and entering locked premises wasn't a crime, not when it didn't profit him, when he was actually the loser by it. His life had been only average blameworthy because it took effort to collect blame. Now he was being made to make the effort.

'Did you see me at the factory? I saw you, I was watching you all the time. I thought you were a girl.'

He was going to be sorry—not about her, what finally happened to her was all the same to him. It was the principle that mattered—that was calling it names, perhaps, dignifying a practically shapeless conviction about his part, what his part ought to be. Not a hero's part, nor a saint's, nor anything the Holy Damned Fraud would own, but a contribution just the same, a plus by virtue of its being minus—Derek Fish's estimate of what was generally not needful. This thing he was about to do came under that last heading, in his estimate there was more than enough of this already.

'I was glad when you came. It gets so dull at the factory and I can't sleep. I'm a half orphan, my grandma lives with us but she's gone to hospital. My father took me to work with him and put me on the shelf so I could hide if anyone came. He says he'll kill me if I show myself and make him lose his job.'

She moved with difficulty in her seat, using her arms to work nearer to Fish. 'I'm glad you're not a girl.'

Fish trod on the accelerator. Driving into the glare of the headlamps was like driving into the horn of a gramophone. The black fields yawned after them and somewhere the black figures of Ritter and Lumley were running away with Fish's money. His nose prickled with pity.

She latched her little sharp chin on his shoulder. 'What's your name, baby?' The car, bucking out of his grasp, threatened to roll over. He clung to the wheel as if it were his mother's arms. 'You *are* shy. You needn't be, I shan't eat you.'

He might have known he would have to go through it as well as through with it. This was only the beginning, she was going to make herself felt and he was the one who would have to feel. He had this genius for feeling and the crime was against him. Ritter and Lumley, the criminals, were forcing him to feel it all.

'Your hair's natural, you don't dye it, do you? I'll tell you something, I didn't even look at those other men, I was too busy looking at you. Anyway, I know your name, I heard it.'

That was marvellous. Here he was, the only one to risk his neck, the one who had to finish the job, who had to feel and who got the smallest cut—and the only one positively identified.

'You're called Goldy.' With an effort that made her gasp she hauled herself across the seat and leaned against him. 'Where are we going?'

Fish had no idea. The road was unhelpful, providing none of the landmarks he could have recognised. Also, it had gone on too long, even allowing for his feelings there was too much of this road. He peered ahead, looking for Hy Cross.

'You're taking me to a dance and I'm wearing a beautiful green dress. When you first saw me in it you said I was like your wildest dream.'

'You're only a kid!'

'How old am I?'

'Seven, six—how do I know?'

'Oh you!' she cried lovingly. 'Remind me to smack your face when we get home and I've taken off my beautiful dress. I don't want to crush it.'

Sight of the village relieved him, he was glad to be on a map, any map. He'd be thankful to be pointed on any pin. Hy Cross, between the moor and the fells, wasn't much of a place, so he took comfort from looking to the west where the twenty-tonners twinkled along the trunk road.

She said soberly, 'Why did you take the money?'

'I didn't.'

'I suppose you want to get rich without working. What are you going to do?'

'I haven't got the money. The others have got it.'

'I expect you'll spend it and then you'll have to steal some more. Will you?'

'No.'

'My father will get the sack. You don't think of that.'

'He should look after the place, that's what he's paid for.'

'Why don't you go to work and earn some money? If you're not clever enough to earn much you should save. I've saved five pounds.'

'Five pounds!'

'Well,' she said, brushing her shoulder where she had leaned against him, brushing off his sin, 'I'd rather have five pounds of my own than five thousand of someone else's,' and Fish was so angry that he blew the klaxon and bounced the noise to and fro in Hy Cross's main street.

'Tell me what you're going to do. What are you going to buy? Will you buy everything you've ever wanted? Will you go away? Will you take me with you? I don't care how fast you go, I can never go fast enough. And I don't want to come back. Let's buy a red, red car and drive like devils!'

How could she be righteous one minute and ready to sin the next—at her own father's expense? She was sickening.

'Where I'm going,' he said, 'where I *was* going, was Vietnam. I had to have money for the fare.'

'What were you going there for?'

'To help. You'd think I'd be allowed to do that!' He saw the track which Ritter had described and turned into it. The car at once began to wallow in and out of potholes. He gritted his teeth as he hauled at the wheel. 'In this world you can't do good, by stealth or any other way.'

'Where are we?' She peered through the windscreen. 'We're in a wood.'

'It's a short cut.'

'Where to?'

'Never mind.'

The track was terrible. Ritter must have meant to fix them both, he meant the car to run into a bog and sink without trace. Or go over the edge of a quarry. Fish recollected hearing that the old workings, under a crust of earth, went down for miles. Coming to these woods long ago on a school treat Fish had discovered that the best treat was dropping stones into a shaft and counting down the splash. Why hadn't he recollected that earlier? Oh little lamb, who made thee to hang on the hook?

'You'll do it,' she said.

'Do what?' He stopped the car, pulled up the handbrake.

'You'll go to Vietnam if you really want to.'

'I just might have,' he said bitterly, 'if someone else wanted me to.'

'Why have we stopped?'

'I'm not going any farther.'

'You're such a baby! Aren't you a baby?' Her white china face looked up at him, in the darkness he felt her smile. 'Anyone can do anything. Don't you know that?' Years ago, when Fish was still bigger than this girl, someone had to convince him nightly that the swarming creatures on the floor of his room were but shadows of the tree outside. 'You've only got to want to enough.'

'Don't give me that!'

'I tell you, anyone can do anything—' and then she sat still and he naturally thought she had paused to except herself but she hadn't. She suddenly and vigorously began to nod, saying, 'I shall walk when I really want to.'

'Can't you see what that makes you? It makes you the can-carrier.'

'I keep trying but I can't do it yet because I haven't been able to altogether want to. It has to be altogether, you see, but every time I try there's something else going on — my hand's itching or my ear's burning. When I really get down to it it'll only take a minute. It isn't much to do anyway — walking,' she said scornfully.

'It makes you solely responsible for the whole kibbutz. Can't you see that? Jesus God!' cried Fish, 'it makes you Jesus God!'

'I'm not responsible for you, silly baby.'

Fish wanted to enlighten her for her own good, as someone should have enlightened him when he was her age.

'If you're praying, don't. No one's listening, there's no one up there except the Americans and the Russians. Do you think they care whether you're fully prayed-up?'

'What are you talking about? I hope you know, I hope the wind's not wagging your tongue.'

'I'm trying to educate you. There's no nice old Gentleman watching out for you, so save your breath. Get up off your knees — if you've got any knees!'

That was her own fault. She had no right to talk like a woman. Her head did not reach his shoulder. She wasn't a woman and she wasn't a child, she was just a living heap.

He told her, 'You make me say things I'm sorry for.' She leaked sorriness. Another day of it and he would crawl into a corner, another week and he would be too sorry to live. 'You ought to know better, the way *you* are you ought to know better than anyone.'

He sat knocking the gear lever in and out. It was time for him to go. He had come as far as he could and the minute anyone sane would have left, anyone with due concern for his skin, had already passed. What was he waiting for? Two courses were open to him, either he could get out and run or he could stay in the car and drive on. Just sitting was not a course, it was lunacy.

Her face broke out of the heap like a whitish flag. 'How you talk! It doesn't impress me one bit.'

'Do you think I'm trying to impress you?'

'I have knees, Mr. Goldy, and I can kneel if I want to. But I shan't because it's such a job. I have to lie flat on my stomach and pull my legs round and get on top of them. And if I don't prop myself I fall on my face. Also I get dizzy on the floor. So what with one thing and another I wouldn't be wanting altogether if I knelt and it wouldn't work.'

'If you think wanting will work it, you're a fool.'

'Oh you! You want everything easy. You've got to help yourself because no one else can give you exactly what you want. No one else knows what you want.'

'Isn't that what I've been trying to do—help myself?'

'Oh you!' she said again, with anger that dwarfed his, 'you helped yourself to the money.'

And their scorn, which had been separate items, melted into one disgust. They sat stiff-necked, despising each other and the world. It seemed there was no other emotion left them, whichever way they turned. Fish even despised himself. She probably didn't go so far, she was very young and had to learn. They sat with the windows shut in their car-shaped scorn.

A tapping on the roof shook them. She fell against Fish in fright and he was hemmed between her and whatever was outside. He expected it to be Ritter, Lumley, or a monster. But when he rubbed the steam off the glass a patrol policeman looked in. He signalled to Fish to roll down the window.

Fish tried to start the engine. He stalled it and the patrolman opened the door. The patrol car slewed across the track behind them, turned up its lights and revealed every bristle on the man's chin.

'Now then, what's going on?'

He would be no wiser if Fish told him. It would take the

gift of tongues and a wide-open mind and this man wore uniform to show that his mind was properly boxed. He shone a torch, travelled it over their faces and bodies and over the inside of the car. The beam waited longest, and well it might, on the girlie photographs stuck to the roof-lining. The patrolman looked at each picture and sighed.

'Nothing.' The word was croaked, Fish's mouth had dried but the palms of his hands were wet. A fierce white worm in the bulb of the policeman's torch turned scarlet, indigo, black.

'Come on now, what are you doing?'

What would Ritter have said? But Ritter wouldn't have stayed talking to the girl, he would have driven her into a ditch and left.

'This is a dangerous place at night,' said the patrolman and she chirped up, 'Dangerous?' She was over her fright, Fish could feel her opening out in all directions.

'There are some old pits round about, most of them unfenced and easy to run into in the dark.'

'We'll get back on the road.' Fish pulled the starter. The patrolman put his knee in the door.

'Is this your car?'

He must know that it wasn't, he must already have its number as a stolen vehicle. Next he would ask for Fish's driving licence, knowing that Fish did not have one. Policemen liked their little game.

'Fancy you bringing me to a place like this!' She reached up and pinched Fish's cheek. She told the patrolman, 'When he gets an idea in his head he doesn't stop to think.'

'What idea did he get?' The torch shone into Fish's nostrils.

'We wanted to be alone.'

'Alone? What for?'

She said in her smiling voice, 'What do two people want to be alone for, officer?' and Fish curled up inside. He heard the frizzle as his last legitimate feeling curled up and died.

The patrolman leaned into the car and turned his torch on her. She was cuddled under Fish's elbow.

'Why, you're only a kid!'

Fish had to laugh although he felt nothing, certainly not amusement. The action started in his stomach and he sat and quaked with laughter until the patrolman dragged him out of the car crying, 'Damn you, she's only a little kid!'

Monstra Deliciosa

MY MOTHER wished me to regard other children as animals and myself as an exception. She blamed my father for the narrowness of my soul. From an early age I was persuaded that my qualities came from her and my defects from him.

'Surely you see how inadequate they are?' She would stand beside me at the window as I watched my friends bowling hoops and rattling along on roller-skates. Inadequate for what? I could only suppose there was an immensely complicated affair ahead of me. 'They are creatures from another world.'

It was a world to my liking and presently, I knew, I would join them in the street. I had to wait while she disburdened herself. This she needed to do from time to time and thereafter would show little concern apart from requiring me not to dirty my clothes.

'Tell me about Damaris.' For I was skilled, as we all were, at exorcising her, and the Damaris method was my favourite and worked better than any other.

She suffered from a special guilt due to not having come up to Expectation. 'Everyone thought,' she would say, 'no one dreamed', and so I had the impression of universal disappointment. My father, a provincial G.P., did not seem disappointed, but his was a blinding cheerfulness.

To me she was an amalgam of mother and child, she was worldly-wise and palpably foolish, to be loved, respected, played along with. Neither aspect of her predominated. Although she was, *au fond*, reliable, her foolishness prevented reliance on her.

She would begin unburdening with the autobiographical statement, 'I was born and bred in London', and follow with the cry, 'Manchester was a savage outpost!' In that nutshell, I think, was her whole discontent.

'When I was a child only slum children played in the streets. We were taken to the park for exercise but we did not scream and race about. It was enough to be in sight of Nature. All those leaves! And grass! And fur and feather—I cannot look at Nature without feeling crushed.'

When I suggested frogs, which were bald, she said that creatures with undisciplined breeding habits were expendable. 'Quality comes before quantity.'

'Did you tell Damaris that?'

'Refinement is what we are here for. It is the purpose of the human spirit.'

To me the human spirit purposed not at all, but perceiving that there was a higher camp, and to have a foot in it, I said, 'We shouldn't be made to learn German at school, all that spitting isn't refined.'

'It is the language of Goethe and Beethoven.'

'They *were* Germans.'

'It is a pity that when you are most fitted to learn you cannot appreciate the value of it.' My mother said sharply, 'You don't even see the need, do you? We must hope this is youth's improvidence and not your father's.'

'Look,' I pressed my forehead to the pane, 'Iris Heathcote has a new bicycle. She keeps wiping the tyres with her handkerchief.'

'Come away from the window. I dislike talking to the back of your head.'

Patience was essential. The therapy could not be hurried. I knew that to get back to my world and my friends' I first must go pretty fully into hers. Half-heartedness would bring on the sort of adult tantrum which ended in my being ordered to my room.

'When Damaris trod on the Bishop's foot—' I laughed as I could unfeignedly do at the story—' he said, "I may not achieve the Kingdom of Heaven but my corns are giving me hell".'

'She was a country girl from some dreadful village where they still burned witches.'

'Did she tell you? Did she see? Oh, I should like to see a witch burned!'

My mother's face crumpled in the same sequence, I observed, as my small brother's when he was about to cry.

'We should be living in Portman Square! You should have had my room with the little balcony. That dear, dear house smelt always of biscuit. You know how cream biscuits smell, rich and sweet and unexceptionably pure? To me that was the smell of purity and I thought of it in church.'

I nodded. 'The blood of the Lamb is sawdusty.'

'The wood of the panelling never lost its fragrance, such beautiful shining wood adding infinite dimensions all the way up the stairs. Such stairs! None of your wooden ladders! It was a free-standing flight—oh it flew up from the centre of the entrance-hall to the mezzanine floor. We had a Turkey-red carpet and crystal chandeliers. When we entertained, the ladies in their ball-dresses floated up and down like swans.'

'*She* floated like an airship!'

'For our coming-of-age we were dressed in Prussian blue silk with silver aigrettes in our hair and bead fringes down to our knees.'

'How funny you must have looked!'

'Striking, yes: distracting, yes: bizarre, perhaps: comic, no.' My mother closed her eyes and raised her brittle nose and the sun pierced it so that the cartilage between her nostrils blazed like a ruby. 'I remember the hush as we descended the stairs. My father told the orchestra to stop playing when we made our entrance. Everyone stood quite still looking up at us and there was a kind of sigh, rustling and then deep, ending in the men's chests. It should have been the loveliest moment of my life.' My mother opened her eyes. 'Hadn't she gone up and down those same stairs enough times to know every inch? Why did she step on the edge and lose her balance? Why never before and never after, why *then*, when everyone was waiting and watching?'

'Why, oh why,' I said, giggling, 'did she have to cry when everyone was listening, "Damn and blast, I've busted my beads!"?'

'She always moved so gracefully, people used to say she was a pleasure to watch. They found her restful. When my brother was ill with malaria he declared that she abated his fever just by the way she moved about his room.'

'Perhaps he was keen on her.'

She glared at me so wrathfully that I was puzzled. 'What language do they teach you? "Keen on her"! How dare you say such a thing!'

She lay down on her couch and turned her face away. 'I despair of my children.'

I knew how to console her. I would pour out a little gin and put the glass in her hand. She wasn't an alcoholic, she had these exposed nerve ends.

'What happened to Damaris? Where is she now?'

'She's gone.'

'You mean she's dead?'

'You could say that.'

'I expect she was like the brontosaurus, too big and clumsy to survive.'

'Run out and play.' She would moisten her upper lip with the gin and pass the tip of her tongue from corner to corner. 'I shall try to rest.'

If the conversation took another course she would go on to tell me about the time they all went on the river. I heard the story on several occasions, told with feeling, always the same angry feeling. The more I laughed the angrier she became.

'It was at Cookham one very hot Sunday in August—no, it

H

was July and rather cold, very cold for July, which made it absurd to have gone on the river at all. But I wanted to, I think I'd have been capable of dying if we hadn't gone. There was something I wanted to happen and it seemed to me that if I could get us in a punt on the river it was bound to. On the river and nowhere else, I thought, it must happen.'

'You wanted Daddy to propose—'

'There was quite a crowd of us, all dressed for a day poling downstream under the willows, boys in white flannels, girls in flowered voile and Italian straw hats. I had a dress of leaf-green silk. My hat hung by its ribbons between my shoulders. I chose everything with the utmost care.'

'What did Damaris wear?'

'She too was in green.'

'Like a cabbage!'

'She had an enormous appetite. It was pathological, she couldn't go on a picnic, even *that* picnic, without worrying that there might not be enough for her to eat. Pies, cakes, jellies, chicken, lobster. "It's not a siege", I told her, but she was horribly afraid something would be left out.'

'Good old Damaris.' I saw both their points of view but more of Damaris's. I too would go on a picnic primarily to eat.

'We drove down to Cookham, some by car, some on motorbikes. He had a sports two-seater. I remember,' she said voluptuously, 'how draughty that car was.'

'Well she couldn't ride with you, she couldn't even have got into it.'

'We had the picnic basket propped in the dickey-seat, she couldn't bear to have it out of her sight. I shall never forgive her for that.'

'Or for anything. But she had nothing else to look forward to, had she? No one was going to propose to *her*.'

'She hoped. Heavens, how she hoped! She kept telling me how he had looked at her, what he said when they were alone. She added up every glance, every word, every breath, every

time he rubbed his nose she made it add up to love. L-O-V-E!'
My mother laughed scornfully.

'You don't mean she was keen on him too? She hadn't a
chance!'

'We were brought up to believe that love was a visitation
and that exactly the same visitation came at some time or other
to everyone. Now I know that love is the expression, the
complete expression of the self. To each his own.'

Although the nature of love did not interest me I did wonder
just how and what she had found out. Especially how, because
it was difficult for me to see beyond the here and now. She
was so inextricably my mother, at the age I was then no longer
the centre but still the just off-centre of my existence. I couldn't
disassociate her from me.

She bowed her head, there was no clue in the rigid winter-
gold of her hair.

'She had as much right as I to expect love.'

'Tell me about the river.'

'How happy she always was!'

'*You* didn't love her.'

'I? I wished she'd never been born.'

My mother had antipathies which were law unto her children. 'I cannot endure', 'I am opposed', 'I dislike', 'I hate' — I
had heard before. But I felt a chill like the chill off stone, off
someone else's dungeon, when she said that.

'She almost capsized the boat when she got in. They made
her sit in the middle, no lying back among the cushions
for her.'

'What about the Plimsoll Line!' I loved that the first time I
said it, but my mother did not smile.

'We were alone, he and I, we were together, nothing else
mattered to me.'

'Daddy must have looked nice in white flannels,' I said filially.

'Your father—' She spoke as if he were that and no more—
'has never worn white flannels.'

'Then what—'

'We floated downstream under the willows just as I had planned. A gramophone was playing, it was a very beautiful day, a hot June day.' Sometimes she said that it was inclined to rain and if I questioned the discrepancy she would ask what could it possibly matter? To me it did. I love a story and it can be the same story over and over, but the details must be the same too.

'He was always very deliberate, he gave me a sense of Fate. Wonderful! As we drifted he knelt before me in the boat and took my hand and said, "The barge she sat in, like a burnished throne, Burned on the water—"'

'What's that?'

'He was a poet.'

'Daddy? He isn't now!'

'It was the most beautiful moment in my life. Nothing could be more beautiful or more wholly mine.' If she had closed her eyes, jealously or tenderly, as often she did, at this point she would cry blindly, 'It should have been longer, it should have been for ever!'

'If she hadn't fallen in the river!' To me that was the supreme moment and each time we came to it I laughed from my stomach. Oh custard, oh pie, I can't laugh like that now! 'If she hadn't tipped up the boat and caused the most horrendous hole in the water!'

'Why should I tell you?' she would say fretfully. 'You know already.'

'Everyone rushing hither and thither, strong men weeping, women fainting, the river bursting its banks!'

She couldn't rise above it, not once could she say, 'That's enough', and send me away. After all, I knew the story and she knew that I knew it and she knew what telling it did to her. Perhaps she couldn't endure keeping it to herself. Perhaps she hoped that one day it would matter less in the telling, or would come out differently.

'There was no fuss,' she said. 'It all happened in silence. Everyone was rooted to the spot. They watched her sink right down to the bottom.'

'She would, of course. Then she'd come up and float.'

'She stuck in the mud, it was very muddy just there—'

'She churned it up. Wopping great Damaris in that little tiny river!'

'It was such horribly brown gruesome mud—'

'It stank!'

'She was covered from head to foot. Her dress, her hair, she had a necklace of mud and the taste of abomination in her mouth. When they pulled her out—'

'And the flood waters subsided!'

'She had lost her shoes, she couldn't walk. They had to carry her along the tow-path.'

'How many men did it take?'

We would be transfixed, I quaking with laughter, she struck raging dumb. At first it distressed me to see the tears on her face, then I realised that they were tears of fury because she couldn't annihilate the world.

My father once startled me by charging upstairs crying, 'Help is on the way!' But it was one of his shouts which he was always shouting and at that precise moment happened to seem to apply.

I knew that he had cherished a weakness for Damaris. I found it incredible and at that stage of my experience resented having to credit it. He had married my mother, I was shocked to think he had looked twice at anyone else.

I said, to give him a chance, 'You didn't really like that old Damaris, she was colossal.'

'She was beautiful.' I thought him unkind to smile on my mother as he spoke. 'A Brünhilde.'

'Was she beautiful when she came out of the river covered in mud?'

'I wasn't there on that occasion.'

'Not there?'

His smile turned on me. 'Large girls don't usually have large eyes. The encroaching fat over the zygomata—the cheekbones—diminishes them. But Damaris had big brown eyes with golden lashes. Very disturbing.'

'Mother's eyes are brown—'

'Child, go away,' my mother said wearily. 'I have a headache.'

'But who—'

'Tea!' cried my father. 'We'll have tea and crumpets.' He took my mother's wrist in professional fingers and felt her pulse. 'The butteriest shall be yours.'

'You know I don't eat.'

'I live in hope.'

She struck off his hand. 'You'll never never see her again!'

As we went downstairs I asked him, 'Do you want to?'

'You've heard the saying that inside every fat person is a thin one trying to get out?'

'That's just a stupid saying.'

'Ah, but in your mother's case she did.'

His natural disposition was to be joyful and I think he sometimes forgot to co-ordinate his face to the moment—I hope he remembered before imparting bad news to his patients.

Noon

PERHAPS no one else appreciated what a decisive time it was because each thought that he or she was the person doing something different. The little ones did not think about it at all, they came from the beach intent on sand messes and scotch eggs, this year they were absolutely dedicated to scotch eggs for lunch. At noon the parents—the 'husbands and wives' Davina Saye-Hennessy was calling them—met together in the hotel bar for drinks; the curtains of the bungalow on the cliff were closed one by one and the skuas flew off their rock for a destination unknown.

Looking up at the bungalow Davina said to Jane, 'I shouldn't fancy it at the same time every day, it's so automatic.'

'Mother says if you make a point of going to sleep always at exactly the same time it becomes as automatic as switching off the light.'

'Animalicule, who's talking about going to sleep?' Davina had grown up since last summer and her amusement was now quite private.

Noon was the time she chose for her sun-bath. She took off all her clothes and lay among the rocks at the far end of the beach, and that too was since last summer. Then she had been a tomboy, salty and ubiquitous. Now she was languid and withdrawn, her rare bursts of energy tumbled Jane as the foam tumbles a cork.

'You can be judged by what you are found to be doing at noon.' Davina scooped a hollow in the sand for her shoulders. 'No other hour is so significant.'

Jane was to be found standing guard although this was hardly necessary since no one else came to the beach at noon. Davina herself wouldn't have bothered but Jane did, Jane fretted.

'Why do you do it?' Even as she asked she suspected that Davina would tell her such a small fraction of the truth as to constitute a lie. 'Don't pretend it's just to get brown all over because I know it's not.'

'Suppose someone sees you?' To Jane that would be as shameful as if someone were to see herself naked on the sand. She couldn't explain but she was furious with Davina for exposing them both. 'What would they think?'

Davina leaned back on her elbows, her eyes shut against the sun. 'You're a damned prude.'

Was that what Jane was? Was it damnable to rather— infinitely to rather—*not* look at naked bodies? And was she permanently damned if she never got to like the sight?

'Don't show how absolutely without it you are, Baby Jane. Nudity is normal.'

'You're only two years older than me.'

'Three. And environment counts.'

'What's wrong with my environment?'

'The question is, are you going to live now, good child, or in the past? You're a hundred years out of date.'

'I am not! I just don't like that sort of thing. I—'

'It isn't any sort of thing,' said Davina, 'it's *my* thing and you couldn't understand.'

'Sitting in the sun makes my head ache.'

'Then go and have nursery lunch with the other babies.'

'But suppose someone comes? Suppose someone sees you?'

Davina may have wanted someone to see her. The thought, coming of Jane's ridiculous concern, interested her. If someone were to see her would she ever do this again? If someone were to see her it would be a conclusion, yes, a logical one, but it wasn't the reason why she stripped, or rather it wasn't the only reason. There were many reasons, all intricate.

She rolled on her face. Here was one: arching her quaking stomach she gently lowered it to the burning sand. With fingers and toes she scrabbled until, under the surface, she found icy cold and wetness. To experience this extra hotness and coldness at the same moment was indescribably important. How could she possibly describe it? Or the feeling that she was full of sea, that she was the quick of the sea, that pierce her and pain would run out into the Indian Ocean? Or the sounds which she did not so much hear as transmit? Which came up through the sand and sounded through her bones? At best they were a kind of music and she the one instrument it could be played on, but generally they were intimations of something else entirely going on. Life at another level. How could she tell anyone that this was her essential private history which poor little Jane would try to forget?

In the hotel bar Tommy Wilsher said, 'This is the best time of the day,' and some of the others agreed. To some the mornings were rather a strain. Their working days were full of occasions to rise to, but the weather had become too hot for golf and unless they were dedicated sea or sun-bathers they had three hours of nothing particular to do. Some of them didn't enjoy that and since they were paying to enjoy themselves it weighed on their consciences and they kept trying to get their money's worth. There should be some keener pleasure than dozing in deck-chairs.

'This is my finest hour,' said Tommy, 'and it's regular.'

'Isn't that a double negative?' his wife said to the Flessatis. 'It cancels itself out.'

'This is when I begin to be human again.'

'It's when you begin to drink.'

'We're on holiday, woman. Aren't we?'

A curious situation when thought about, and a few of them

had thought about it while watching the sea rolling and un-rolling. Lots of time, food, drink and scenery were the authorised version of bliss but some one or two of them had heard a voice crying, 'I don't know what more you want!'

'Tommy's been on holiday all his life,' Netta Wilsher told the Flessatis, 'which is not such an achievement because nothing kills a holiday so stone dead as having everyone else kicking around too.'

'You don't know anything about me,' Tommy said to her. 'After fifteen years of marriage you should have picked up a few specifications. For one thing, I like people, I need them. With people I come alive—'

Netta laughed. 'I've done my best,' she told the Flessatis. 'I keep coming in in different hats and I say "rhubarb, rhubarb, rhubarb" to encourage him to talk—like mothers say "wiss, wiss, wiss" to get the baby to go pee-pee.'

'People!' shouted Tommy. 'I need warm-blooded human people, not a cold tin bitch!'

'What are you drinking, Netta?' said Ellyott. 'Gin and french?'

'I'm not drinking. We can't afford both to.'

'Am I hearing right?' Tommy appealed to the Saye-Hennessy's who came into the bar then. 'Or am I stoned already?'

Netta stood up and with a Huckleberry gesture dived both hands into the pockets of her jeans. 'This morning we're three gins to the good and that's thanks to me.'

'Do I beat you? Or starve you? Do I go to another woman for satisfaction? I don't know the meaning of the word any more—'

'Be quiet, Tom,' said Mrs. Saye-Hennessy. 'We've had a long, long morning on the beach and we've come in for some short, short drinkies. No sexual recriminations, please.'

'We're not drinking. My wife says we can't afford to. Will the barman give a rebate on this whisky which I've only looked at, or can I interest any of you in a second-hand Scotch? At auction—going, going—in a good cause—to keep my wife from starving.'

'Netta's drinking with me,' said Ellyott.

'She can't accept charity. She's got principles, she's got them all over. I tell you, hedgehogs don't have prickles where she has principles.'

'It's not charity—'

'That's how there can be little hedgehogs!'

Ellyott put his hand on Netta's shoulder. 'It isn't charity, it's my privilege and pleasure,' and steered her on to the balcony. She was trembling but her smile was tight. 'We'll make it a large gin,' he said.

'I haven't even got the excuse that he's drunk.'

'He is in a way. After a drink or two he'll sober up.'

When he came back from the bar she was gazing out to sea, her chin in her hands. He was glad to see that the smile had gone and she had stopped trembling.

'We heard a strange sound last night,' she said. 'It was about eleven o'clock, we were walking along the beach and the sea was very dark—you know how enormously dark it can be. We were very happy. We often are,' she assured him sharply as if he had questioned it. 'We heard something, I can't describe it but it was low and sweet and we stood still to listen because even the shuffle of our feet on the sand drowned it. Tommy said it was mermaids singing.'

It never ceased to surprise Maurice Ellyott what men said to women, how out of character it was. He put the gin into her hand. 'This is a haunted shore.'

'Is it?' she said, 'Is it?' as if it mattered. Perhaps it did, if she wanted mermaids she would want ghosts.

'I suppose one can expect it of any shore—if one is disposed to expect anything of the kind. Not, perhaps, of Brighton beach, though there have been drownings even there.'

'Isn't that your Jane?'

He shielded his eyes and looked. The small dissolving figure in the heat haze was unmistakably his Jane, unrelaxed as a squirrel, on a big loaf-coloured rock below the headland. He smiled at the Janeness of her.

'Tommy blames me for not having children,' said Netta, and he was brought back into the thick of that.

'Tommy doesn't want children,' he said. 'He told me.'

'He doesn't want them as such—if you know what I mean.'

She drank half her gin and twitched the base of her glass round and round on the stone parapet. It made a slight gritting sound which emphasised for Ellyott the unpleasantness of the incident.

'I think women over-estimate the importance of procreation to a man—the function, that is, not the act,' he said carefully. 'They are congenitally unbalanced on the question. I think a woman is more likely to blame herself, often quite unjustly.'

He was also thinking about Jane. Why was she there? She was passionately inconspicuous by nature, sitting alone on a rock on a deserted beach in the noonday sun wasn't like her.

Netta said, raising her glass to him, 'Thank you, Ellyott-with-a-y,' and he complained to his wife afterwards about people who asked for sympathy and then mocked the sympathiser.

'She wasn't mocking,' said his wife. 'She once told me she envied me. "Your Maurice is stamped right through," she said, "like a stick of rock".'

'I don't care for her analogy.'

'Oh my dear, take it from whence it came. Netta can't trust Tommy even to handle their domestic finances. Do you wonder that she envies anyone with confidence in her husband?'

'I didn't care for Wilsher's, either. Some things are private and incommunicable, it's embarrassing when people try to communicate them. I resent being given innuendoes to translate.'

'Don't you think she felt that too? She was grateful to you for stopping it.'

'I hope they don't make a habit of it, I shan't make a habit of my part. By the way, what was Jane doing on the beach at noon?'

'On the beach?'

'I saw her from the balcony. She was sitting on a rock, all alone.'

'Alone? She usually goes with Davina. Today I was too busy with the babies' lunch to notice what she did.'

'What I find surprising,' said Ellyott, 'is the time and place. The beach at noon is an odd place for Jane to be.'

'She really should have her lunch with the little ones and take a nap while we have ours. She shall tomorrow.'

But by tomorrow Jane had a blinding headache and sickness and was so miserable that she lay in a darkened room and wished to die. The light hurt her terribly. It was stored up in her head and broke into scalding splinters except when her mother's hands covered her eyes. The doctor diagnosed a touch of the sun.

'She's delirious,' said Ellyott. 'She's had more than a touch, I should say she's had a thump of the sun.'

'She appears to have something on her mind,' agreed the doctor. 'Can't you reassure her?'

Jane's mind indeed seemed to be giving her as much trouble as her sickness. Her face was pinched with worry.

'Don't go to the beach, Daddy, don't let *anyone* go to the beach.'

'But Jane, they're all on the beach, as happy as sandboys.'

'When they come up,' said Jane faintly, 'don't let them go back. Promise—'

'But why, Jane?'

She was about to be sick again and wailed in her misery.

'Just promise,' his wife said sharply. 'That's all you need do.'

'How can I?'

'Because the child's ill and she asks you to!'

So Ellyott promised and Jane leaned retching over the basin.

'Poor little sweet,' said her mother, 'she's worried that the others might get sick too.'

Ellyott doubted that. He was not denying his daughter's goodness of heart, he was remembering the outline of her on the rock. Why did she sit up there as if to the crack of a whip?

His wife laid the child on her pillows and gently touched the wide-open eyelids. 'Rest now, darling, everything's all right. A promise is a promise.'

Jane looked at her father. He was not to know what passed between them but it seemed to satisfy her and her eyes blinked shut as tight as a doll's.

There was nothing more that Ellyott could do. He went slowly downstairs, pausing on the landing to look through the medallion window at the sea. He took these pictures with him when he left, these locket pictures of a small sea—the depth of glass it was, perhaps, that minimised it. On choppy days the foam creamed along the shore, in calm weather the sky and sea were cracked with a fine hair crack and the boats, when there were boats, inched along the radius and vanished. Ellyott liked to remember the views from the landing window. He had formed the habit of stopping to add to them whenever he could.

It was now eleven o'clock, the sky was white hot. Red and blue children like confetti were dotted over the sands. Sighing, Ellyott went downstairs and out on to the terrace. He noted that they had just watered the paving stones and swept them. The stones steamed as he watched. Really it was unseemly and if he had wanted brass heat he could have gone to Spain.

He found a chair in the scant shade of a wall. Here, everything was battened down, pinned back and put away from the wind and rain, there was no provision for prolonged heatwaves. At night now, after days of unmitigated sun, the old rocks sweated but did not completely cool. Ellyott's trousers dragged at his damp knees as he sat down, he picked them up between finger and thumb and shook them free.

He could only suppose that Jane in the blaze of noon had meant to mortify her flesh. Since she was of his flesh he had some idea of what she had suffered. Children, other children, were primitives. He excepted Jane, but he knew that she was devoted to her principles and some of them, necessarily, were childish.

Tommy Wilsher shambled past wearing wet bathing trunks and a sandy towel over his shoulder. Seeing Ellyott he came back and flopped down beside him.

'Got a cigarette?'

Ellyott gave him one and Tommy hugged his knees and smoked strenuously. He had plump round knees covered with golden fuzz like babies' heads.

'Don't believe all you hear.'

'I don't think I've heard anything,' said Ellyott.

'She—Netta—told you I was a drunken sod.'

'No.'

'That you can believe. I am. But I'm not bankrupt.'

'She didn't say you were.'

'She'd like me to be, she'd like me really down in every way so she could raise me up. Women all want that.'

Ellyott could see that it might be true in Wilsher's case. Whatever he did to himself he looked like a damped and tidied boy.

'I can't complain about the profit margin. In my line of business it's never staggering, but it's steady.'

'That's nice,' Ellyott said politely.

'I daresay I'm worth as much as anyone here. I *do* say it!' Pink rushed up out of Tommy's collar into the roots of his cornstalk hair. 'I'm worth more than Saye-Hennessy on his Army pay and Flessati with his pickle-works.'

'Flessati's in the wine trade.'

'And he drinks on an expense account. And his Mercedes is a company car. Well I couldn't live like that, what's mine's my own.'

'It's odd weather we're having for this part of the world,' said Ellyott. 'This long hot spell has changed the character of the place.'

Tommy glared. He looked maternal with those twin baby heads clasped to his bare chest.

'I could lend *you* a card or two.'

'No doubt.'

'You're full of doubt!' Tommy's rage suddenly gave out. He flung himself on his back with a winded grunt. Looking up at Ellyott he was a size smaller but had become privately content with himself. 'You're right to be. And Netta's right to watch our outgoings, though God knows what good it can do. We wouldn't be here if she weren't paying, she said we had to have a holiday. "Let's try to get back where we started, let's try to be friends again". Friends! What the hell does she mean?'

Even Tommy did not expect an answer to that. He employed himself smoking his cigarette upright like a funnel and making train noises. Ellyott flexed his damp knees preparatory to getting up and going.

'We never were friends. I used to tell her as much as I thought good for her and the fact is, nowadays the less she knows the better.'

'I assure you I've forgotten the incident. I imagine everyone else has too.'

'Poop, poop!' said Tommy, and moved his arms like pistons.

'Excuse me. I find it uncomfortably hot out of doors at this time of day.'

'You're excused, old Ellyott-with-a-y.'

'Why do you call me that?'

'Because it's your name.'

Ellyott went back into the hotel. His wife was not in their

room. She looked up when he gently opened the door of Jane's room and put her finger on her lips. Jane was sleeping.

The time was eleven-thirty-five. Ellyott lay on his bed and watched the clock. He heard them come from the beach, the children first—their voices like the chatter of sparrows on Sundays. Then came the adults, the Flessatis hauling their fibre-glass boat over the pebbles and Saye-Hennessy who cracked his towel like a whip, all of them who kept the noon ritual.

He lay until the door slammed on the last voice. He heard the skuas go over, circling round as was their custom before flying away. Then he put on his hat and went down to the beach.

He and Jane were much alike. She had her principles which were sacred to her, and horrors which he recognised as young versions of his own. He grieved sometimes for the offences which she would be caused. She was going to grow up to a series of shocks, a blow-by-blow destruction of what she in her innocence held dear. He wished her a thicker skin and a less passionate heart.

The spring tides had thrown cordons of pebbles up the beach. They were like mountain ranges, the valleys between being deep enough not to be able to see over. Ellyott, standing at the bottom, watched the peaks bleed off into the white sky. He began to see the same sly motion everywhere, it was all slipping in the heat. He could smell dead crabs and stranded fish which would undoubtedly have reached a high degree of putrefaction. His tongue tasted foreign to his mouth, but he was scrupulous in his repugnance. He picked up and fingered the texture of one of the pebbles. It was sticky with salt. He put it back where he had found it and climbed on up the slopes, lifting his feet as if to negotiate eggshells.

Jane must also have disliked this. She would have disliked it more, tender Jane could not have expected to enjoy herself alone in the wolfish heat of this utterly inhospitable place.

I

And if she had found herself here by accident she could have upped — the word was appropriate to her manner of departure — and left. Why hadn't she? Why not, with the glare making her head throb and the smell and feel unpleasantly affecting her? His hope of finding out was minimal because probably Jane herself could not have told him. Probably it was incommunicable.

When he should locate her rock he proposed sitting there himself — briefly, he stipulated, wiping the triangle between his upper lip and his moustache — he would then either see what she had seen or, if great minds think alike so surely must blood-related ones and he would get an idea how her thoughts had tended.

He didn't find Jane's rock because he found Davina first and it was a measure of his dislocation that from then on he scarcely remembered Jane's part. He thought at first that Davina was a mermaid. They exist! he thought, without tenderness or enchantment. But the idea did have significance and seemed, even in his confusion, to presage radical alterations.

He was horrified. In a fractional moment he experienced fear, revulsion, dismay — and indignation on account of supposing her a monster half human, half fish, which would create confusion in scientific circles. There was also the implied insult to the human form.

He objected to being personally involved with such a discovery. Mermaids were not only legendary creatures, they were seaside low comedy, picture postcard jokes of the order of the fat lady in a striped bathing-suit.

Then he saw that she had two legs like everyone else. She lay with her head towards him and her feet to the sea and her face being upside down it was by her long poker-straight hair that he recognised the Saye-Hennessy child. He groaned and stirred in his stiff clothes.

Davina had heard him coming over the beach. She had been

unsurprised, knowing that he must come. The end had been ordained—if that was the word and was not merely what was done to clergymen—from the beginning. She had to be seen, Heaven knew why—Heaven must know, no one else did.

Calmly she turned to look, not particularly concerned about identity. But when she saw that it was Jane's father she was furious. Hell, she thought, oh bloody damned hell! Aren't there any *people* here, only parents?

She glared up through her eyelids. She wasn't going to move or try to run away, anyhow she couldn't now without his seeing her. Perhaps if she lay still he would politely look the other way. He was a very polite person. Where was he going? Down to the sea for a private paddle while the beach was empty and no one would see his bare feet? He never swam or sunbathed, he sat in the shade in his linen suit doing crossword puzzles. In Davina's unconsidered opinion he might as well be dead except for the use he was to Jane. His footsteps over the pebbles sounded like a horse munching. Davina, wondering what Jane would make of the development, sniffed with laughter.

The crunching stopped suddenly. She arched her neck and looked backwards. He was about twenty feet away, at the top of a ridge of pebbles and though he wore dark glasses she knew that he was looking straight at her. No man had ever done what he was doing, not even her own father. What a foul trick of fate that someone's *father* should be the first!

'Go away! Shoo!' she said aloud, but of course he went on looking through his medicine-blue lenses, he probably thought she didn't speak English, probably he thought she was a big blue shrimp.

She relaxed her neck muscles and lay flat again. Apparently things could go wrong even when they had not been planned, nor sought, nor entirely understood. What she meant was, there had seemed to be a reason for what she experienced on this beach, it had all seemed to be getting her somewhere. How

stupid and pointless and stultifying if it had to end with Jane
Ellyott's father.

Ellyott feared she was going to scream. He would suffer
complete disintegration if she did. At present he was shattered,
though not widely, and held himself together, just. Seeing
her mouth move and open he waited with skin crawling. But
she uttered no sound, or none that he heard. She flattened on
the sand and the soft-shoe shuffle of the sea, passing for silence,
kept him from falling apart.

After a physical crisis people need just to sleep. He needed
just to look. He realised that if he were to get decently by this—
he could never get over it—he must be allowed to look. He
stood as sharp and still, had he known it, as Jane on her rock.
He didn't give Jane a thought, not Jane or anyone, with Davina
shining full in his face.

The naked women he had seen in rooms, among beds, chairs,
tables and the universal tooth-glass, had not prepared him for
this voluptuous child on a stark white shore. Remembering
those women wouldn't have made her any easier to look at.
He did not remember, he gazed like Adam on his converted
rib.

Davina was going to be big. Her mother had told her, 'Men
like big girls and Army men prefer them. Remember, it's the
men who matter, I'll not have a girl of mine left on the
shelf.'

'What a quaint phrase. Lots of people don't believe in marriage.'

'You do. And you believe in God.'

'What's God got to do with it?'

'It's part of the same thing.'

'I may not stay in the Army,' Davina had said. She meant
to have a career, she wanted to taste all sorts of life—eventually
she would have to eat some of it. 'I'm not interested in men
per se.'

'What?'

'As distinct from women.' But Davina's mother maintained that she would be when the distinction became apparent. Davina privately contested that, and on the beach with Mr. Ellyott considered that she had disproved it. In the first analysis, Jane's father was a man.

She remembered the bottle which Alice had found in Wonderland, bearing a label – 'Drink Me'. She needed no label, the sun drank her up through to her backblades and when she turned on her face she was dry as a leaf. Mr. Ellyott stood absolutely still, as still as death. She felt a twinge of interest.

Ellyott had been holding his breath. When she moved he allowed himself to exhale. The sun leaned on him and sweat ran over his lip and down the backs of his legs. He noticed nothing. He was simply a seeing eye, seeing the girl tapered solid as a fish from her waist to her upcurled toes. Seeing her for five minutes? Ten? He could not have gone farther or forgotten more in a lifetime of travelling.

He came to himself as if a switch had been pulled. Davina heard him leave. She did not lift her face from her arms. Punch, punch, punch! went his feet on the pebbles, walking away fast.

As they sat at lunch Ellyott's wife asked him if he had found anything.

'What should I find?'

'When you went to the beach.'

'I went. Why not?'

'I was wondering why Jane was so anxious that you shouldn't. I thought you might have found out.'

'I went to find out, if I could, why she should choose to stay there until she made herself ill.'

'Netta Wilsher says Jane regularly sits on the beach at that time of day. She can see her from her window. When the heat's really unbearable, Netta says, there's Jane bolt upright on a rock.'

Ellyott found that he preferred not to think about Jane on

the beach. He preferred not to think about the beach at all.

'She won't tell me anything,' said his wife.

'There's probably nothing to tell.'

'I shall ask Davina Saye-Hennessy if she knows.'

'It will be best if we simply drop the subject. I don't believe it will happen again.' At the moment of speaking, he did not. It was unquestionably an isolated incident. His wife stubbornly crumbled her bread. 'It will be kinder to say no more,' he said, rebuking her.

Davina, at table with her parents, considered Mr. Ellyott through her sunglasses: as from this p.m. she had taken to wearing them indoors. She found him better-looking than the other men, though not nicer: Ted Cotterell was nicer looking but he almost always overdid everything and this Davina found pitiable. Jane's father was actually handsome, actually his paternity was irrelevant she now realised. He was not as much a parent as her own father—or as Mrs. Ellyott for that matter.

He has redeeming features, she thought, looking at his profile, he has not coarsened himself with family living.

He appeared uninvolved even with Mrs. Ellyott—or *particularly* with Mrs. Ellyott. Although he sat at a table with her they did not make a pair.

He did not look at Davina, not once, not even in her direction. It would have changed the whole complexion if he had. Tommy Wilsher would have looked at her, had it been Tommy Wilsher who saw her nude on the beach he would have brought her nudity right back into the dining-room with him. And expected to flip the secret between them. Tommy Wilsher would wink and wave, she could picture him waving two fingers at her across the tables.

'Take off those glasses, Davina,' said her mother. 'It's harmful and rude to wear them indoors.'

I suppose it could have been worse, Davina thought resignedly, laying aside her glasses. Without them she saw that Ellyott's cheekbone, where his beard would be if he did not shave, was lavender blue.

Next day Ellyott discovered that he was prepared to go to the beach at noon. He stood patiently in a corner of the terrace, a non-shady spot but one of the few places where he would not be noticed. He would not allow himself any reaction, he was like a man with a tricky beast which needed to be given rope before it could be finger-tip controlled.

People were still spread among the rocks and bobbing about in the sea. It seemed impossible that the beach would ever be vacated.

The old Downeys were the first to move, they had weak hearts and could not hurry. Then the Cotterell boys went, kicking a beach ball, and Saye-Hennessy strode up from his swim. The children ebbed and flowed and finally leaked away and at the cliff bungalow the curtains were drawn over the windows like the thin eyelids of a bird.

Who had instituted the exodus? Was it only this summer, an uncharacteristically hot summer, that everyone got up and left the beach together? Why did they do it? Not to escape the heat of the day, many were back on the beach by two o'clock when it was appreciably hotter than at twelve. Just to drink or to get ready for lunch or because, like the children, they were made to?

He saw Davina wearing a green dress and walking among the rocks and so sharply turned from the sight that he pulled a muscle in his neck.

Perhaps last year he simply hadn't been aware of the exodus at noon. Perhaps there was no significance in common, perhaps it was simply a habit which everyone happened to keep to and any time now someone would break.

He began to walk slowly down the beach over the intrusive pebbles. He did not wish to intrude. Once he saw a green flash like a flag among the rocks and went cold with anger.

But he kept on, lifting and gently placing his feet. The noise of the stones lacerated him.

Davina thought, I shall never understand why I did not understand that it had to be him. There's no other possibility, they're all too old or too young. He stands out like a sore thumb — no, not sore, he's too collected, and not a thumb, he's a long middle finger.

She remembered how Mr. Ellyott had looked at her on the day she arrived at the hotel. When she went in to dinner he had put his chin on his hand and looked, but he hadn't seemed to see her after that. He's seeing me now, she thought.

She hadn't been sure that he would come to the beach again today. Suddenly it had begun to matter, before she could turn around it mattered intensely. When she undressed last night she could see no reason why he should come. She wasn't the shape yet. Her breasts were like kitchen cups, they should be pointed like pears: she couldn't keep her stomach in, it positively pouted, and she had almost no shadow between her thighs.

If he did not come to the beach and she did, she would have to live with the knowledge. There was a distinct possibility of its poisoning her life. Then she saw him waiting on the hotel terrace, wearing his bread-coloured suit and his cap. He was so *fully* dressed!

He came down the beach and stood in the same place as yesterday, already she thought of it as his position. He has taken up his position, she thought, but of course they were not playing a game. At least not a children's game. She believed it was the word 'play' she objected to.

Ellyott had gone through the time between, through meals, conversations, encounters, appearances of rest, pretences of sleep and gestures of habit, passing the hours until noon. Everything he did, appeared to do, was cover for that — yet it wouldn't have mattered, either, if there were no cover, he believed he would simply have come to the beach and looked, or simply stayed on the beach and looked. Simply, simply, was his cry from the heart.

And looking was so soon unbearable. The glare hurt his eyes. He shut them and girl-shaped blood blazed under his eyelids. He opened them and she was glutted with light.

So much ultra-violet brought on prophylactic tears. He did not attempt to rub or blink them away, he turned and climbed blindly back up the beach.

He asked Saye-Hennessy, 'How old is your daughter?'

'Davy? Going on thirteen.'

'She's – tall for her age.'

'We're all tall for our age. I'm six foot three, my wife's five-nine and my son's six foot four and a half.'

He delivered the information with zest. Ellyott sensed that it was an integral part of his philosophy.

'Davina's bright with it,' said the Major. 'Tell me, is it still waste to educate females?'

'Still?'

'It always was. And biologically they haven't changed, they've pushed themselves but they're still the only ones that can proliferate.'

'Excuse me,' said Ellyott, but the Major held him with a plain stare.

'I don't think women are inferior, I think their minds are different. No daughter of mine's going to be educated beyond her capacity.'

Ellyott averted his eyes from the tuft of hairs in the hollow of the Major's throat. He had hoped the confrontation with Davina's father might restore his sense of values, but he found himself unable to accept that the girl on the beach had the remotest connection with Major Saye-Hennessy. He could not even connect her with Davina Saye-Hennessy.

'She'd make a good nurse, she has the brain to count swabs and the brawn to lift the incontinent sick. She wants to be a doctor, of course.'

Davina Saye-Hennessy was still a child. Dressed, even partially, in that avid summer, he recalled that her body was not serene. It filled out her clothes like soft fruit filling out a paper bag.

'Or a lawyer because she can argue the toss.'

The girl on the beach was more original than a child and she had existed long, long before Major Saye-Hennessy.

'It's important to know your limitations.' The Major complained to his wife afterwards that Ellyott's expression — when his face had any — did not synchronise with what was being said to him.

In the morning the sea had a skin which did not break even on the last wave up the beach. All along the shore it lifted and lapsed without a crease. There wasn't a cloud in the sky and it was hotter than ever. The black hand of the barometer moved backwards when the glass was tapped.

Ellyott watched them go to the beach. The small children were fretful and buffeted each other. Their wails mixed with the cries of the skuas which could not settle on their usual rock.

'The weather's breaking,' said old Mr. Downey as he came by. 'The birds know.'

'It's not that,' Tim Cotterell told Ellyott. 'There's a hawk about.'

Hand in hand the Wilshers passed Ellyott without a word. He watched them walk into the sea. Their heads remained precisely the same distance apart.

He played clock golf with the other Cotterell boy. After several rounds Ted Cotterell suggested a swim.

'No. I am definitely not going to the beach today.'

'Well, I am.' Ted dropped his shirt and trousers on the terrace and vaulted on to the beach. He already wore his bathing trunks.

Jane was much better, she was sitting up in bed, reading. Mrs. Ellyott had had rather a bad time with her.

'Nursing a sick child in a hotel, one is made to feel like a criminal.'

'I suppose they were afraid she might have something catching.'

'Like Bubonic Plague?'

'Why don't you lie down for an hour before lunch?'

'What I'd really like is a drink. Jane won't need me for a while.'

Ellyott looked at his watch. 'No one will be back from the beach yet.'

'They really have been disobliging about Jane. The trouble it was to get her a little iced water! With children in the place there should be some sort of room service at night.'

'I suppose a hotel must run on the assumption that everyone will be normal.'

'Every morning I had a fracas with the chambermaid. She wanted to turn out Jane's room and if I hadn't been there she'd have turned Jane out with it.'

'We shan't come here again.'

'But you like it here.' She too paused at the medallion window on the landing. 'So do I.'

'There's no need to make a habit of it.'

'None of the children have ever been ill on holiday before. It might not happen again.' She said, looking through the window, 'How much more pleasing a view is when it's framed.'

'I admit it's a very clean hotel,' she said. 'The girl was telling me she has to turn out every room every other day. Thoroughly. The manager's Swiss and of course there's no other work for people here.'

'We shan't come back.'

He had a whisky while he waited for noon. When the time came he stood up and put his bar stool into place and announced to his wife that he was going for a walk.

'A walk?'

'Why don't you come?' He was without compunction.

'This is the hottest time of the day.'

'It gets hotter later on.' He touched her hand in leave-taking and left her at the bar.

'Maurice!'

He did not look round although he smiled at Netta Wilsher as he passed her.

He was so prompt that Davina hardly had time to undress. She threw off the last of her clothes and lay back on the sand as he came round the rocks.

She had to hurry for him but good heavens, she thought, she had him in the hollow of her hand. Did she want him there was not the question. Mr. Maurice Ellyott was a secret if ever there was one, her own father did not know what he thought about. 'Is he clever by any chance? Is that what's the matter with him?'

Mr. Ellyott came at her bidding, a man of thirty, forty or fifty. She could have been born and died three times at least in his life-span. He came at noon because she took off her clothes at noon: if she chose to take them off at some other hour, in some other place, he would come just the same. He would come running. Between yesterday and today was this difference: yesterday he ran away from her, today he ran to her, crash, crash, crashing over the beach regardless.

He was behind her in his position, waiting before the last pebbles had ceased to slide from under his feet. They were suddenly both dead still, like lizards flickering and freezing into immobility.

Her own heart was beating from somewhere it certainly couldn't be—in her throat or her head—but there was no sound from him. He was noiseless, odourless and she could probably call him 'an acquired taste' of life. This morning the sea was quiet too, easing into the land with no more sound than the water in a swimming-bath after the last swimmer has climbed out.

No doubt she could have fainted from just whatever came into her head at that moment had she been fanciful or nervous. She stretched herself taut and with her fingers began secretly to dig for coolness under the burning sand. By pressing back her head and pushing up her chin she was able to see his face. Today he wore no hat and no sunglasses, he was staring at her with black eyes, somehow he had lost the whites of them.

He took a step nearer. The relief was enormous. She had been afraid he would do nothing. There was nothing *she* could do and they could be struck like this for ever on the beach at noon.

One step at a time he lifted his legs and set his feet down with infinite care so as not to disturb the pebbles. He looked so funny and bread-coloured, bread suit and bread face and two burnt currants in his head. Did he think he was deceiving her? If she sprang up and cried 'Boo!' she could reduce him to crumbs.

A little avalanche ran down from the crest of the pebbles. She stopped herself from crying out as something hit her face, she must not frighten him.

He *was* frightened, he froze into stillness, his foot lifted, waiting for the subsidence to cease. Davina, with her neck arched, watched him upside down. This she had to see. It occurred to her—she liked to see in the round—that the scene was set. The quiet sea and the empty beach had been setting it all morning. She felt like a patient wheeled into the operating theatre where everything has been got ready and she wanted to stand up and shout 'Crumbs!' but she knew he would not crumble.

He lowered his foot, negotiating for somewhere to put it, moving with fearful deliberation. When he reached the shelf of pebbles immediately above her he began to tremble as if the weight of the world were on him. His hands met and locked on his chest—Davina had seen men contending with their two right hands, each hand straining to bring the other down, but these were his own hands contending with each other. Under the weight of the world he broke up above her very eyes. Bits of him floated down, his jacket first. His jacket dropped over her and he climbed back up the beach.

Useless if Dropped

THE first I heard of Ilona Paull was that she was dying. They would want me to take her place they said, they were very frank. To her they explained that I was engaged to look after the foreign rights, she had enough on her hands with home sales they said. That was twenty-five years ago and Ilona is still alive—I shan't say very much alive because she has never given that impression.

She has some obscure disease of the blood which doctors find fascinating. They are always having her in for tests and comparisons, they use her as a practically indestructible guinea pig.

'The game now is to see what will finish me,' she says.

She still looks dreadfully frail and I still find myself trying to let her down lightly, tempering the wind for her. Then I realise that she is forty-five years old and the flame of life doesn't flicker that long.

The strongest thing about her is her hair, it is beautiful and abundant, once it was the colour of cherished gold. Her skin is still the colour of low grade milk, bluish-white.

When she was young I couldn't imagine her looking older: we all thought it would have been an academic exercise anyway because we believed she'd die any minute. In fact she doesn't look older to me now, she only looks more like she ought to look.

She has no figure, just enough flesh to identify her bones. I often wondered what men felt about her physically: the idea of using such a painfully mortal body for sex was repellent.

But she attracts men and it isn't only their protective instinct she arouses.

When I met her she was working for Franconi Films, a company which operated on a shoe-string. The shoe was Lewis Franconi's and what money there was in the business he put into it. I think if he had been good at business and not so good at making films he would have done better. He spent his money anachronistically, on equipment when it should have gone on wages, storage when he could have hired, location expenses when he could just as well have shot around the corner.

Ilona was constantly comforting people who hadn't been paid or weren't being paid what they thought they ought to be. I had to too, but I was never able to be as comforting as Ilona.

Franconi made short features and documentaries and advertising puffs and was trying to get into television. 'Foreign rights?' Ilona said to me, 'What foreign rights? We have none. Never mind, we'll take turns making the coffee.'

But there were times when she couldn't get to the office. 'It's this damned thing,' she'd say faintly over the phone and everyone shook their heads and told me she was a very sick girl.

In her absence I had to do Lewis's letters and sit in on his thought. He was a melancholy, irascible man who could ignore you, or rather me—I never actually witnessed it happen to anyone else—for weeks and then pin me down on some throw-away remark. He made me so nervous I couldn't even read back my shorthand.

'What have I said?' he'd ask. 'No, before that—no, no, no— what? Why didn't you say you weren't getting it down? Oh God, you're not going to cry!' And of course when I wasn't, that would start me off.

He liked to think aloud and it took a very acute or loving perception to know when his thoughts were for committing to paper and when he was simply marshalling them. 'I didn't dictate that!' he'd cry, 'that's nonsense, no one but a bloody fool would say that!' and he'd glare at me, for who else was there to have said it?

He sometimes sighed, he was a most expansive sigher—he had such a big resonant nose—and turn his back and go to the window. Or he might worry the sentences out of me one by one while he filled and lit his pipe. He was marvellous, too, at expressing irritability with his pipe, he couldn't have expressed more if he'd played on it. 'Look here, this isn't the way to draw up a contract. Did no one ever show you?' No, no one ever had and I was frightened stiff lest I should bond someone to something or ruin the Company with a sin of omission. 'Ilona always does the contracts,' he said, 'get her to do it.'

'But she's not here—' I thought he must have forgotten. 'She's ill—'

'She's not dead. Yet.' He gave me an impacted stare which confirmed what I had already sensed. He felt for Ilona a lot more than was humanely necessary.

And Ilona? It was only the other day that I knew she had feelings. For twenty-five years she's appeared to do nicely without and to my mind it's seemed right that she shouldn't have them—on top of everything else I mean. And there are always one's own to be considered.

I don't mean that she's unsympathetic. Far from it. Ilona is kind but indiscriminate. Her kindness lacks direction, it just emanates and I thought she was spared love. Nature, I thought, wouldn't require her to feel what she could not implement.

'Lewis likes you,' she'd say to me. 'You mustn't mind his Poeness, he'd really be unhappy if there was nothing to be gloomy about.'

When I was introduced to Estelle Franconi she said, 'I'm so glad you're going to help Ilona. We want her to rest more, Louie's such a dream when he's working, he wouldn't notice if she died on her feet.'

It was a tactless remark and I tried to cover it. 'I'm not much use yet, I don't know the first thing about films,' but Franconi pinned me with 'If you did, you'd be no use at all.'

'Ilona must bring you to supper next week. Our old friend Peter Ledoux is coming and I'd love to have him meet you.'

'Thank you, but I don't know—'

'Thursday? Do say you can!'

I said I could because of the way she asked. 'I know I'm not important, it was nice of her to pretend that I am,' I said to Ilona afterwards.

'Don't be so modest.'

'I know I'm no use, he didn't have to tell me.'

'He didn't tell you. But he would if it were true. At least he's honest.'

The 'at least' I recognised as an indication of Ilona's attitude towards Estelle Franconi: she was prejudiced I thought.

Besides Peter Ledoux there were half a dozen people at the Franconi's the night I went to supper, all of them with money or influence or both. I thought that Ilona and I must be the only two having neither, but it turned out that I was the only one without.

When I arrived I found Ilona lying on Estelle's bed.

'Estelle insists on my resting before dinner,' she said and turned her face into the pillow as if it were her own. In that unrequiring way of hers she did seem to be in complete possession. There was a loving nucleus, a family cosiness between the Franconis and Ilona. I suspected something of a *ménage à trois*—which, I thought, would mean that Estelle was accepting it on her terms and those two were taking it on his.

Peter Ledoux sat next to me at supper and I remarked on its being quite the family affair. 'Except for me,' I said. 'I don't belong.'

'But, my dear, you're the newest member. We're all united in devotion—' he had a falsetto voice and did not trouble to lower it—'to this dear, sick girl.'

I saw Ilona looking at him and crumbling bread in her fingers. She was smiling, she had certainly heard. So had Estelle who leaned forward and tapped his plate with her knife.

'Do you like the paté, Peter?'

'Enormously, my sweet.'

'You have Ilona to thank for that.'

'Thank you, darling Ilona!'

'If she hadn't come to my aid you'd have had no dinner at all,' said Estelle. 'The cook is prostrate with toothache, Ilona and I toiled all the afternoon to feed you.'

'I worship you both!' cried Ledoux and passionately kissed his fingers. To me he said, 'Estelle is devoted to Ilona and so is Lewis. So, of course, is Lewis.' He was either unable or unwilling to modulate his voice. It carried all round the table and his whisper was piercing as he added, 'It's an act of mercy.'

I suspected that Ilona was often with Lewis, more often than not, I suspected. When I invited her to my place for a meal in the evening or at weekends she'd accept and then wander into the office we shared and say in her implacably gentle voice, 'I can't make it after all, I'm afraid.' If I asked why, she'd say vaguely, 'I've got to see someone', and if I then asked who—as I made a point of doing because I dislike my arrangements broken—she'd say, 'A friend', and I'd have to drag out of her what I could of the friend's age, sex, business.

Once she said, 'Lewis is bringing some scripts to discuss', but thereafter when I asked she'd say it was no one I knew.

I had no idea what Estelle's terms were but she was obviously happy with the relationship. She was always coming to the office, into our room, Ilona's and mine, and Lewis would join us if he was in. She brought cartons of chicken in aspic from the Corner House and half flagons of burgundy to fortify us against Lewis's moods and she would stand behind him and hold his head on her breast and tenderly stroke his eye-·lids.

Everyone was happy and trusting, I found so much trust hard to take. I told them that I wasn't hungry, wine made me bilious, and tried to lose myself in my work. I had no work to do anyway. After I heard Estelle actually entrusting those two to each other I looked for another job. I could see that I wasn't helping Ilona and I couldn't help Estelle.

She came one cold, wet day fretting about Lewis who was determined to go to their cottage at Twyford for the week-end. The cottage was damp, in this weather everything would be wringing, she said, and she couldn't see to it because she was having people to stay, people Lewis did not like. That's why he wanted to go to Twyford.

'He won't look after himself, he'll sit fireless reading scripts and eating condensed milk and bullaces.'

'In peace,' he said.

'What about my peace? I'll be wretched thinking of you, and when you come back I'll catch your cold.'

'It's too early for bullaces.'

'Condensed milk alone will be worse.'

They both looked at Ilona as if it were her turn to say something. She said it, 'Don't worry, I'll go and cook his supper.'

'Oh darling, you're an angel!' Estelle declared to me, 'Isn't she an angel?'

When we were alone I told Ilona that I thought she was a fool.

'Why?'

'For one thing, it doesn't sound a healthy place for you.'

'And for another thing?'

'Estelle worked at it.'

'Worked at it? Oh, I see. Perhaps she did, she really doesn't like the country.'

'Do you?'

Ilona's humour is effulgent, like her kindness: she uses it mercifully to blunt the point of any matter. 'Yes, I like walking in the rain and wet cobwebs and sheets that smell of toadstools.'

* * *

Years later, when I hadn't even been introduced to Edgar Hardwick and we had only started to talk to each other because we went to pick up the same brochure at the same moment, I heard of her again.

The brochure lay on the floor, you pick up brochures from the floor at a successful, noisy cocktail party if you're not being successful and noisy yourself. This glossy pamphlet about Ribjoy Digressives lay rather nearer to my foot than to his. We dived for it together, impelled, I suppose, by the same guilt at not being seen to be talking or listening, and having only our empty glasses to sip from.

He held out the brochure. 'I beg your pardon.'

'It doesn't matter. I thought someone might trip. If you're going to read it—'

'I was going to look. New, isn't it? This is the first I've seen. There's probably an advance copy waiting for me in Bradford, I came away before it arrived. We're last, in the Regions, to see these things.'

'Oh, Bradford.'

'Do you know it? Actually I live out of town. In . . .' People were making such a noise that I didn't catch the name. 'You won't have heard of it, no one has. It's named after a big estate which existed from Domesday times. All gone now, the house and grounds carved up, there's just the name left.'

'What is the name?'

He leaned towards me, raising his voice and enunciating. 'Edgar Hardwick, area manager for the North Riding. I haven't had the pleasure—'

'Alice Soutar.'

'David Soutar's wife?' He looked surprised. 'I'm pleased to meet you.'

'Could you get me another drink?'

'Of course.'

When he came back he drew his chair beside mine. 'Is your husband taking this New York job?'

'He hasn't been offered it yet.'

'I can't.' He sucked in his breath sharply. 'Absolutely no question. I told them.'

'You turned it down?'

'It's an important assignment, all-important to Ribjoys, breaking entirely new ground, a whole empire. It requires an empire builder, a soldier, a diplomat and a spy. All in one.'

He could be the soldier, he looked like a major — Major Hardwick. 'Which of those aren't you?'

Again he breathed in deeply, through his nose this time, filling his chest. 'I have circumstances, Mrs. Soutar.'

David, in the centre of the floor, was doing his imitation of a man with a fruit machine. It was going well, the managing director was roaring with laughter.

'Your husband has no doubts.'

'Oh, David's always like this. He loves being with people. I don't think he's given New York a thought. There's so much competition for it.'

'About you, I meant. He can be sure of your co-operation.'

Hardwick carried a battery of pens in his breast pocket where medal ribbons would have been, and his wrists were the bony wrists of a trier, they made the glass he held look frivolous.

'As I see it, the post requires a married couple. Whoever goes to New York must have a wife he can depend on absolutely, who has his interests and the interests of the firm at heart, who is able to serve with all her strength. There can be no passengers.'

'Oh, it could be a lot of fun.' I hadn't thought about it either, I didn't want to and I believed there was at least one good reason why I needn't. 'David won't get the job. He's too new to administration, he's only just come off the road.'

'Fun, Mrs. Soutar? You don't think that. You know as well as I do that you've got to sell yourself. No one but your own mother takes you without persuasion nowadays. Ribjoys are mortgaging their existence to open up in America, sacrificing prototypes that haven't yet seen the light of British day—'

'Well I don't know anything about that. And I don't know what part a wife could play other than cooking and washing and listening—which she does everywhere under the sun.'

'Of course, of course a woman's work is never done.' He lowered his voice. 'A well woman's work, Mrs. Soutar—' He added, with coy sorrow, '—a sick woman's is never begun.'

David had finished his story. The managing director was wiping his eyes, the managing director's wife lifted David's hand high over hers like a referee declaring a winner.

'This sort of thing,' said Hardwick, 'this social scene which you grace equally well, I am sure, as hostess and guest, is immensely important in the States. The New York agent's wife will have to give parties, formal and informal—showers, don't they call them?—join sororities and clubs—golf, bridge, fencing, literary, charitable—there's no activity the American woman doesn't go in for. A wife can impede a man's career or nip it in the bud if she cannot cultivate the wives of his business associates.'

'David likes to do his own cultivating.'

'He'll need your understanding, everything is different over there.'

An old song started churning in my head: 'Over there, over there—' Like Ypres or Mons, because Major Hardwick would be a World War One soldier.

'David hasn't got the job. He won't get it.'

'Someone will.' Hardwick rolled his empty glass between his palms. 'Someone who has a wife to stand by him.'

'Is there no Mrs. Hardwick to stand by you?'

'There is and she would – until she dropped. She soon would drop, God help her.'

'You wouldn't have to fight Indians you know, the covered wagon days are over.'

'My wife is dying, Mrs. S.,' he said briskly, and we sat there, both as red as bricks, and he made himself redder by carefully stooping and stowing his empty glass under his chair.

I muttered that I was sorry, I hadn't known –

'I try not to inflict it on people, it is my burden,' he said.

And hers I thought, surely. 'If you took her to America there might be something they could do, some more advanced treatment –'

'That wouldn't be honest, would it? Digressives wish to send out a ball of fire, not a sick woman and a distracted husband.'

'Oh damn Digressives!'

He leaned his wrists on his knees and bowed his head. 'There is no further treatment, the disease has nearly run its course.'

'You mustn't give up hope.'

'We've bought all the hope there is. We've paid for it. Specialists' fees, clinics, nursing-homes, drugs, that's what the "cost of living" means to us.'

The managing director had his hand on David's shoulder and was oaring him through the press of people gathered about the Chairman of the Board.

'That's what making a success of life means for me,' said Hardwick.

David managed to turn and wave to me across the room. He completed the gesture by holding up his thumb. Hardwick saw it.

'There, didn't I tell you? He's got the job.'

I couldn't believe that it could be so easy, even for David. But later he took me aside to confirm it.

'They're going to make an announcement. We'll have to look suitably starry-eyed.'

'Yes.'

'You're pleased, aren't you?'

'Oh, my dear, congratulations—' It was an achievement. His rise had been meteoric, only eighteen months previously he had been a door-to-door salesman.

'But how do you feel about it?'

'I'm glad, of course I am.'

'Living in America—are you glad about that?' He was looking at me searchingly. He knew I had worries and I knew that he thought they were groundless. He thought it was just my dread of the new and strange. He didn't know that I was shocked and panicked and frightened stiff. Or if he did, he thought he could fix it for me.

'I'll do my best,' I said.

'To be glad? To like living in New York?'

'To do my part of the job. The social part. I know it's important for you.'

'Relatively.'

'And not very easy,' I said, 'for me.'

'Rubbish.'

'I could fail you. With the best will in the world I could be simply not good enough.'

'Don't be an idiot.'

'I haven't been good enough for you here—oh I know that!—so what hope have I got over there?'

His face changed, became quite blank as suddenly as if I had touched a switch turning off David, my husband, and turning on a basic stranger. I knew then how much he wanted the job.

I cried, 'You let me think it was just a question of living there—you didn't tell me how much I'd be involved!'

153

'How could I? I've only just got involved myself. Anyway, you needn't be if you don't want.'

'I do want. If it will help the slightest, smallest bit I'll give suppers and lunches and bridge-parties and join clubs and charities. I'll learn fencing and golf. Edgar Hardwick says—'

'Hardwick? So you've talked to him.'

'He told me what to expect. That's why he couldn't go to America, it would be physically impossible for his wife to take any part.'

'Hardwick was never in the running for the job.'

'He told me—'

'He told you that his wife's a hopeless invalid.'

'Isn't it true?'

'Certainly. He's made it his career—or his reason for not having one.'

'I think that's fine of him.'

'Sickness has toughened her. She can stand worse things than you or I can, she's had to. Ilona Hardwick will outlive us all.'

*　　*　　*

She probably will. I saw her yesterday for the first time in twenty-five years and David was right. Sickness had denuded and strengthened her. She is herself complete, non-essentials have gone and only the structure remains.

There had been a scene with my daughter Erlys. A theatrical scene which Erlys acted in. She is seventeen and thinks she is adult, she thinks she was created that way. She grows so fast, every week something is left behind. She thinks she's outgrown me. It would have happened anyway but the pace I blame on her American upbringing, the pace and the lack of mercy.

We quarrelled about the state of her room. I am tidy by nature, muddles upset me. Here in London we have only this small flat which if it isn't kept in order is no better than a burrow.

I was about to pick up after Erlys, I've done it often enough in the past and I knew that she was in a hurry to go out. But she began pretending that it was absolutely vital that everything should stay like it was. I had picked up one of her shoes which she had kicked off and was looking for the other. She took it out of my hand and put it back on the floor, deliberately placed it on the spot I had taken it from.

'Leave it, I want it left.'

I told her if she meant to put the shoes on again directly it would be helpful to have the pair.

'I want one here and one over there, just as they are.'

So I asked which dress she was thinking of wearing because I'd get it down for her and put away some of her other things at the same time.

'This is my room!'

'Of course it's your room,' I said, 'I'm just trying to help. You surely don't want this mess—'

'I do! I want this mess, I want to keep this mess. I may make it bigger.' She reached into the closet and dragged out some of her clothes, still on hangers, and heaped them on the floor.

I tried to laugh it off, though really it had gone too far for that. How could it have gone so far so quickly?

'This will be something for me to do while you're out. I'd planned to go early to bed for a cosy read—'

'Leave my room alone!'

'Erlys, please stop acting.'

'I am not acting. This is my room and I don't want it touched.'

'But your nice things are tumbled on the floor. Your new trouser suit—and you know how suède shows every mark—'

'Will you please let me alone?'

'You say you're no longer a child but your actions betray you. Only a very young child would behave like this.'

'Mother, if you won't go—now—I shall.'

'Surely not, darling, in just your panties and bra?'

I managed to smile. It wasn't easy, but I thought if we smiled together we'd get out of this not too scathed.

But she did go, then and there. She snatched up a coat and ran out of the flat. I believe she didn't even have shoes on. I checked her shoes afterwards and they were all there.

I ran after her, down six flights of stairs and kept seeing her spiralling away from me. When I reached the ground she was gone into the street.

Erlys has been difficult since her father died and I have to expect rebuffs, but this was heart-rending. It rent my heart to shreds. And my God, it felt final.

I went back and tidied her room. I picked up her clothes, I put her shoes on the rack and set everything in its place on her dressing-table. I wiped up the powder she had spilled. I vacuumed the carpet so that it was absolutely clean and then I laid out the dress and shoes and accessories she'd been going to wear. I always do that for her. I even emptied her handbag and brushed out the lining and put back her things in the order she'd need them, purse and taxi-fare on top ready to hand. There was no key to the flat in her purse so she probably had it in the pocket of the coat she'd picked up.

I was too upset to relax. You've got to wait, I told myself, she'll be back directly and you must pretend it never happened. Don't seek a showdown, not tonight, anyway.

I walked round and round the flat, couldn't keep still. When I realised she wasn't coming right back, she was going to let me fret, I suddenly got angry and walked out myself. I wasn't going to have her find me so disturbed by what she had done. I had nowhere particular to go and couldn't kill enough time just walking so I got on a bus. There I met Ilona.

She was sitting opposite, smiling her wry, gentle smile.

'You still run after buses,' she said, and it gave me quite a pang. I had supposed that smile to be dust and ashes long since.

'Ilona! What on earth are you doing here?'

Here on earth I should have said, or more exactly – how do you come to be doing here at all?

She was thinner – as a girl she did have some tender outlines – and altogether darker. Her hair, which used to be gold, was dyed chestnut and the hollows in her face had changed from lilac to tea-brown. She lived a war of attrition and the thought struck me that if she were suddenly and miraculously cured of the disease she would die of the peace.

She had a room in Sheldrake Gardens. Yes, she was a widow. 'So am I, since last year.'

'I thought you were in America.'

'I was until David died. How did you know?'

'Someone must have told me.'

'The last I heard of you was from your husband, ten years ago.' Major Hardwick – I must still be cherishing the memory of the little sherry glass in his big trier's hands. 'What happened?'

'He had an accident with an electric razor.'

As I said, Ilona's humour is diffused, one doesn't know where it's directed or even if it's humour. The thought of Major Hardwick doing that small thing for himself and doing it wrong amused me but I certainly couldn't assume she was sharing my amusement when she smiled, slightly wry and inflexibly gentle.

We talked until we reached her bus-stop. I got off too and suggested we find somewhere to have a cup of tea and talk some more but she said no, she ought to be getting back.

I stood there, loath to lose her company. She rather hesitantly invited me to go with her to her place and I said I would, just for half an hour. Erlys would be home waiting for me, I said. 'She's a child still, I don't like leaving her alone.'

'What does she want to do?'

'Do?'

'When she leaves school.'

'It won't be for another year. She has a drama-fixation at the moment.'

'A what?'

'She wants to be an actress. It's absurd.'

'Why?'

'For one thing, she's not the type.'

'And for another?'

'I wish you wouldn't say that! She simply isn't right for the stage or the life.'

'Mrs. Worthington,' murmured Ilona.

'What?'

'This is where I live.'

We had arrived at a sawn-off Victorian terrace. The rest of the houses I supposed had been demolished.

She went up the steps of the end house. 'Mind the top tread, it's apt to tip.'

I'm thankful to say I haven't been in many places like that. I began to feel sorry and shamed—why shamed I can't imagine, unless it was something to do with Digressives treating me better than they had obviously treated Ilona.

The house was awful, built-in ugliness gone to seed. The chocolate-brown plaster was chipped off the arch in the hall and the iron banisters were rusted. The glass panel on the front door coloured the air cabbage-water green.

'Don't lean on the banister rail, it isn't safe,' Ilona said cheerfully.

She had to be poor to live in such a place.

She pushed open a door on the first floor landing. It wasn't locked, anyone could have walked in. And if she thought there was nothing worth stealing she was right. I've junked better furniture than any in that room. And it was so untidy, book and parcels of books everywhere and jigsaw pieces on the floor and the ashtrays full and posters pinned on the walls and mobiles twisting and pot plants trailing and I vow the rugs were made of carpet samples tacked together.

Ilona said she would make tea and she went through to a sort of closet to fill the kettle.

I wished I hadn't come. The muddle upset me, I felt as if someone had taken a stick and stirred my insides up. Well, Erlys had done that, but I was also very conscious that on top of losing her husband—which had been too much for me—Ilona had to be mortally sick and poor into the bargain.

I ought not to have found out, after all there was nothing I could do about it, nothing I could usefully feel.

'Do sit down,' said Ilona and cleared a chair by tipping the books off. 'I'm doing research for a social conscience writer. It pays the laundry bills.'

'Didn't Edgar—his job was pensionable, wasn't it?'

'You know what percentage of her husband's salary a widow gets from Digressives. Edgar wasn't senior staff.' Ilona smiled. 'We're all right if we don't all change our sheets the same week.'

'All? I thought you lived alone. God, what's that?'

Someone was hitting the wall with what sounded like a sledge-hammer.

'Only Oonagh.' Ilona went to the wall and rapped twice. There followed three mighty thwacks from the other side. 'That means she'd like a cup of tea. She's about a hundred years old, and bedfast.'

'Who looks after her?'

'We all do.'

'All?' I said again.

'Oonagh invented a knocking code, it's possible to hold quite a conversation but she's deaf and thinks everyone else is. I don't know if the wall will stand up to it.'

'What about you? Can you stand up to it?'

'I have a charmed life.'

I looked about me while she made the tea. If there was charm in living like this I couldn't see it. But I wished Erlys there with me for a moment, long enough to look and tell me truthfully if this place had charm for her. It had certainly been 'left alone', it was near the logical outcome of being so left. Surely Erlys would forgive me if she saw this. Forgive me? Forgive *me*?

I called to Ilona, 'David said you were tough.'

'He was right.'

I should imagine the boy slipped in sideways. When I saw him he was flat against the wall, easing the door shut with his thigh. We looked at each other. I was rather alarmed by his stealth and more so because it was patently absurd if he thought he could get in without my seeing him.

'Who are you?' I said. 'What do you want?'

'I live here. You don't.'

I felt like saying 'Amen to that'.

'May I know your name?' he asked politely.

'Alice Soutar.'

At once he bawled at the top of his voice, 'You didn't tell me Alice Soutar was coming!'

'I didn't know she was coming,' said Ilona, bringing in the tray. 'We met by chance after—twenty-five years, isn't it?'

'We met by chance,' said the boy. 'Ilona and I.'

Ilona said to me, 'He lives upstairs. His name is Peter Panetti.'

'Please, no comment. May we take it as made?' He sat on the floor facing me. There was a hair-tautness about him which I found tiresome. I thought him conceited.

'I live upstairs but I'm almost always here in this beautiful room.'

I looked at him sharply. His manner annoyed me, so did his unremitting stare. I wanted to talk to Ilona about old times and perhaps about present ones.

'Whatever happened to the Franconis?' I said.

Ilona was pouring tea and did not seem to hear. She gave me a cup and put a mug of tea into his hand. I was the only one to have a saucer.

'Oonagh wants tea. I won't be a minute.'

When she was gone he leaned towards me. 'Isn't this a beautiful room?'

'You should try blinking more often, it would relax your eyes.'

'Thank you, I will,' and he sat squeezing first one eye shut, then the other, preciously holding his mug in both hands. I disliked him.

Ilona came back smiling. 'Oonagh didn't want tea, she wants an orange with the top taken off and a piece of sugar put in. What code can we have for that?'

'If she's bedridden,' I said, 'how do you cope?'

'She's very good, she doesn't knock unless it's really necessary. And for company of course. We all keep her company.'

'She reads to me,' said the boy. 'She has a fine reading voice, like a foghorn.'

'Hasn't she sons or daughters to take her?'

'None of us has sons or daughters. We're alone and friendless.'

'Alice has,' said Ilona. 'She has a daughter,' and Panetti said, 'She'll never never be alone and friendless, will she?'

Ilona happened to drop a knife. It fell beside his foot but he didn't attempt to pick it up, he sat and watched her grope for it.

'Erlys is very immature,' I said. 'In America children become sophisticated but they don't grow up. She relies on me for everything.'

'We rely on each other,' said Panetti, as trustworthy as a wet paper-bag, and fluttered his eyelids at me.

'How have you been?' I asked Ilona. Sitting there peeling the orange for the old woman she looked tired to death. One day she's going to die and with her it could always be tomorrow. Yet she allows people, selfish people, to advance the day.

She smiled. 'As you see me.'

'She sees you a picture of health!' cried Panetti. 'We're all pictures of health.'

'I'm glad you think so. Ilona—'

He shouted, 'We're as healthy as navvies!' and spilled his tea.

'Of course we are.' Ilona took the mug from him. 'He hates to think of anyone getting ill,' she said to me.

'We're fitter than fiddles!'

'I shouldn't like to disillusion him,' I said, 'but for your own sake—'

'I didn't finish my tea, I want some more. I have a healthy appetite. And Oonagh's hungry.' He thumped the wall with his fist and the answering wallop brought down a drift of plaster. 'She wants pork chops. I want sausages and beans. Isn't it time to eat?'

'When Kate and Homer come.'

'If you're expecting people,' I said, 'I'd better go.' I was disappointed at not getting Ilona to myself.

'Kate and Homer live here,' she said.

Panetti chanted softly with his mouth full of biscuit, 'Ilona's little Kate. Like mother and daughter they are. They don't have to be the same flesh and blood for that. They don't even have to be the same colour, Mrs. Soutar.'

'This Kate and Homer, are they married?'

'Homer would give his soul to be! There are two little snags. He has a wife and Kate doesn't want him.'

'Do be quiet, Peter. Alice doesn't want details.'

'It's none of my business,' I said to her, 'I'll come and see you some other time.'

'Don't leave it too long. We may not be here. This house is due for demolition.'

'Heavens! What will you do?'

'Find somewhere else.'

I looked at her, mistrusting the active verb. To drift, she meant, trickle, leak, end up somewhere else. I have always thought of Ilona in passive, pervasive terms.

'We're going to live in the country,' said the boy.

'I have a spare room in my flat—' We're liars when we speak such literal truth. The room that's to spare is bigger than those four walls, sometimes I get panicky and think it's as big as the wide world. 'You could come and stay until you've somewhere to go.' She wouldn't, of course, and I was furious with her for the refusal I felt in the air. 'I'd look after you. You need a rest.'

She smiled her gentle abstract smile and thanked me.

'You'll come?'

'We're going to live in the country.' Panetti lowered his chin on his chest and spoke almost in a whisper. It was not put as a question, he wouldn't bring himself to ask but he was sounding her out none the less. His comfort was at stake. For the first time since he came into the room he wasn't staring at me and I felt completely in the round again.

There came a crash so almighty that it shook the glass in the window-frames.

'Oonagh wants to know if we're still here.'

'She'll have to go into hospital,' I said.

Ilona smiled at me. 'She brings the plaster down, we have to dust her off every night.'

'I should certainly see that you got a rest.'

Sometimes I can't rest because of all the room there is to spare. Sometimes Erlys doesn't come home and the flat's like the cave of the winds. I lie awake—not that I'm nervous of being alone, it's the actual cubic space that haunts me.

'You're trying to separate us.' The boy lifted his eyes to me. 'That's what you've been sent for, haven't you?'

'I haven't been sent.'

'Everyone has a talent, I didn't know what mine was until your people started coming. You can't deceive me about you.'

'My people?'

'There have been one or two Welfare visitors,' said Ilona. 'The house being due for demolition they got concerned about Oonagh.'

'I'm brilliant at identifying you,' said Panetti, 'through any disguise.'

'I am not in disguise and I have been a friend of Ilona's for twenty-five years.'

'You could say that, you could say anything and she'd believe you. But to me you're obvious—'

'Come any time,' I said to Ilona. 'The room's always ready.'

'You've got foreheads like writing-desks and noses like button-pushes.'

I do have the trick of pressing the tip of my nose with my thumb when I'm vexed and having it remarked on vexes me more.

'I don't have to like this sort of thing even if he is crazy.'

'Stop teasing, Peter.' Ilona turned to me. 'He doesn't mean anything personal. He couldn't, he's blind.'

It seemed to give him the advantage. I looked into his wide open eyes and there was a clear gap between the membrane and the iris, like under the dome of a bubble, but I didn't believe he was without sight.

'I want to be with them,' said Ilona, 'with Oonagh and Peter and Homer and Kate. We've agreed to stay together wherever we go.'

Panetti held his head sideways as if to hear a chime of bells. 'Oonagh's old and I'm blind and Ilona's sick and Homer's lovesick and Kate's black and we'll be together always.'

Glory, Glory Allelujah

W HEN Joan Brown had seen off the last of the mourners she returned in time to hear her friend Helen Wicks, Helen Lipton that was, asking what they were going to do. Darby said he supposed there would be some adjustments and then they would go on living.

'Naturally,' said Joan.

'Will you? Naturally?'

'We always have.'

Helen laughed. 'As naturally as caged rabbits.'

Darby Brown looked to his sister for help. Helen had dismayed him since the first time Joan brought her home to tea, an ageless schoolgirl then, with life already conquered. She was no worse now that she was married and most of the time she was better because she lived far away.

Joan was reminded that she had cried during the service and went to check her face in the mirror.

'I haven't seen myself since seven-thirty this morning. Black doesn't suit me.'

'Darby looks hot. Why don't you take your jacket off, Darby, or your shoes, or whatever's pinching you?'

'I'm rather tired, that's all.' Although he and Joan were twins and similarly, if not identically, minded, they had points of departure. Like this permissiveness towards Helen Lipton. Joan took anything, she always had, from Helen. 'It's been a tiring time.'

'We've not been caged,' said Joan. 'I think it might have been better if we had been.'

Darby knew what she meant but Helen Lipton didn't.

'Then why didn't you break out?'

'There was nothing to break out into. At least I couldn't see anything and I daresay Darby's gone as far as he wanted.'

Helen asked him, 'How do you like teaching?'

'Very well.'

'You find it rewarding with all those young minds to bend?'

He wondered if she knew that they were backward minds, he had no intention of telling her.

'You'll stay to supper of course,' said Joan.

'My dear, I can't. I hate driving in the dark and I shall have to start back at once.'

'Then have some coffee before you go. It won't take a moment.' Joan went away, leaving him unsupported.

'Well, Darby, it's all over, including the shouting.' Helen Lipton lit a thin cigar and slightly smiled round it. 'There'll be no more of that, will there?'

'She was very quiet — finally.'

Words had finally failed their mother, but only at the last hour and she had still done her best to be audible. He remembered the groaning and blowing out of her lips and at the very end a furious quacking which had upset Joan more than anything.

Pale blue tendrils from her cigar now began to pretty the air round Helen's head. She was a decorative smoker.

'This place,' she said and sighed with impatience, regret or amusement, he couldn't tell which. 'Every time I come here the same thing happens to me — you may not believe it, but I'm twelve years old again.'

Darby didn't believe it. She had been a grown woman all her life.

'Mother didn't want anything changed.'

'But you will, won't you?'

'We shouldn't know where to start.'

'My dear, you must start with the walls. All this ginger paint is stupefying, you and Joan are getting comatose. Perhaps there was some excuse for her as the only daughter—though it's not one I'd make for myself—but what have *you* been doing?'

'If I tell you the story of my life,' he said, in desperation trying on her the twinkle he used to reassure the smaller, frightened boys, 'you won't get home before dark.'

She blew him a smoke ring. 'You once asked me to marry you. Remember?'

'Did I?'

'On your thirteenth birthday. You were worried about getting old and lonely.'

She had no scruples and was at liberty to say anything.

'Do you know what your mother said the last time I saw her?' Smiling, Helen made a bud of her lips. 'She said you would never marry while there were so many little boys about.'

'I'm afraid it's going to rain. We can always tell, this slab in the hearth changes colour when pressure falls.'

'Doesn't it worry you now—the thought of getting old and lonely?'

'I think being young and lonely is worse. I teach at a school for backward boys.'

'I know. I think it's admirable.'

'Did Joan tell you?'

'No, your mother. She thought you and Joan were both admirable. The "pigeon pair" she called you.'

Joan couldn't see it, she thought this woman her friend, she couldn't see that they and their mother and their home were a kind of *olla podrido* for Helen Lipton.

'I shall never forget her. As a matter of fact I met a man who had only seen her once, in court five years ago, and he said he'd remember her the rest of his life.' Helen put aside her cigar and set to work on her face with the compulsion of a cat starting its toilet. 'There was a touch of *Wind in the Willows* about that episode.'

'What episode?'

'Poop, poop!'

Darby knew what she referred to. At seventy their mother had bought a huge old Daimler. She ignored rules that did not directly benefit her and drove about the country on the crown of the road at thirty miles an hour, stopping only to get out, or for manifestly adamant things like walls. There was a summons, then another, and before either could be heard an encounter with a coke lorry which had found the Daimler parked in the middle of the road immediately beyond a bend.

Liza Brown had appeared in court in her own defence. No one discovered what her defence was to have been because she chose delaying tactics, challenging every statement, including the statement of her own identity, until the business of the court had to be done—as someone put it—'not sub-judice but sub-Liza'. She lost her case and won the day. There hadn't been a session like it in living memory.

'My mother had principles.'

Helen smiled. 'Poop, poop.'

Of course Helen Lipton had enjoyed herself. Darby remembered his chagrin at seeing her in court and furiously asking Joan how Helen could have got to know that the case was up for hearing. He had still hoped that someone or something could intimidate his mother and that she would let the lawyer take over her defence or, better still, plead guilty. But it was only an attempt to bolster his morale because he knew that she was going to put up a show. He wasn't prepared, however, to see her guy herself and her family.

'I always meant to ask,' said Helen, 'why she turned up in court in a crash helmet?'

It had been one of the few times in Darby's life that he had been tempted to kill. 'Will no one stop her?' he had thought—but he was the only one qualified and capable. When he saw his mother enter the courtroom in that track-rider's helmet and heard the murmur of surprise and laughter he was eminently capable.

'Have you no charity?' He turned his back on Helen. 'She was an old woman, troubled in her mind. Can't you allow her a harmless eccentricity?'

'Troubled in her mind? Your mother? She was a great deal less troubled than you or I. Don't be such a stick, Darby. She had a fiendish streak and you know it. I think she did it to spite you.'

'She's dead, isn't that enough?'

Helen pressed a tissue to her newly made lips. 'Dying's the one thing that's never done by halves.'

Joan, coming back with coffee, was in time to hear that. She put down the tray and tweaked the cups straight in their saucers. 'Is that supposed to be a joke?'

'My dear, it's a trying time for all of us —'

'Not for you.'

'When it happens to me it tries me and it does happen to us all, you know. Sooner or later we lose someone —' Helen Lipton paused to blink her dry eyes — 'dear to us. You don't have to tell me what it's like. When Granpa Wicks died I was absolutely lost. He'd lived with us for years so it was like losing a limb.'

'Mother was the root and branch,' Joan said.

Darby was thinking that black really did not suit her. She had a khaki-ish skin which needed colour. He recalled, bitterly, a comment of their mother's: 'Joan's string and you're straw. Why couldn't I get one good dummy out of a single birth?'

'Of course she was,' said Helen. 'All mothers are.'

Joan had meant a lot more than that. The worst of it was — and it was the crux of the present situation — that Helen Lipton knew, roughly, what Joan meant. So did everyone, everyone at the funeral this afternoon could have taken Joan's meaning. So that he and Joan looked ridiculous and everything they did looked ridiculous, every filial thing, every decent sober step they took to the churchyard, every penny they spent on the ceremony.

'Darby was saying you'll be making changes,' Helen said smoothly. 'If you want my advice you'll start with this room and do it over in white and Wedgwood. You'd be surprised how revivifying the right colour scheme can be, and I do think blue and white would be right here. All these visceral reds — you can't disembroil yourselves.'

'Mother liked this room.'

Brother and sister looked at each other. They realised that that was no longer a reason and that as an excuse it was invalid. They also felt, between them, an uncertainty which each had supposed a private weakness of his or her own. Sink or swim together—well, they would have realised it sooner or later. Darby blamed Helen for hustling them.

Perhaps Joan did too. She added, 'We have a lot to think about.'

Helen drew at her cigar, exhaled, and briskly stubbed it out. 'My advice is to act first and think after. You two have a lot of time to make up.'

'Have we?'

'You talk as if we've been let out of school,' said Darby.

Helen smiled. 'My dears, come off it. You know the danger better than I do, or you should. Anyone who christened her children "Darby" and "Joan" was writing you off from the start.'

'What do you mean?'

'Stop teasing him, Nell.' Joan went to the window and opened it, letting in the smell of ivy. 'You're going to have a wet drive home. We can always tell —'

'The stone on the hearth changes colour when it's about to rain.' Helen pulled on her gloves. 'My dears, if you're going to say the same things at least say them to different people.'

*   *   *

'I think she enjoyed herself,' said Darby as they watched her drive away.

'She means well.'

'She'd like to remake us in her image.'

'Because she thinks it's a good one?'

'Obviously.'

'A moderately successful image is Helen's ideal. She thinks that too much of even a good thing is vulgar. At school she despised those who came top of the class as much as those who came bottom.'

'If we enumerate Helen Wicks's, née Lipton's, moderate success,' said Darby, taking up his blackboard stance, 'we find it comprises one husband, two cars and three children. And a month at Porquerolles every year.'

'George Wicks has a thriving business I believe.'

'As a cattle-cake manufacturer.'

'Well there'll always be cattle and they eat a lot of cake.' Joan stacked the coffee cups on the tray and retrieved a piece of sugar from Helen's saucer. 'As Marie Antoinette's poor would have done. I don't see anything wrong with it as a way of making money.'

'Do you envy her?'

When Joan Brown smiled it came as a surprise, even her twin couldn't be sure what would motivate the muscles of her face.

'No. I'd rather be at the very top or the very bottom.'

'She thinks we should change everything.'

'Everything *is* changed.' She was still smiling, to Joan a smile was an enterprise not to be lightly abandoned.

They had been careful not to declare themselves openly to each other. Careful, although they knew each other's minds and really had no need to declare. They also knew that an improper declaration, too open or too early, could offend and offence could become a wound. Careful, yes: they had reached a delicate moment in their lives.

'Piggott was in the churchyard, hiding behind a grave-stone.'

'Not hiding, surely?'

'He's taken my point about not being welcome. There'll be no more whisky nights or days.' Darby sounded her with a sigh but she went on pleating the skirt of her unbecoming dress, letting the pleats jump out and starting again. He said sharply, 'That's a change for the better.'

'Helen asked me how Mother died, what sort of end she made, how long it took, what she did.'

'You didn't tell her?'

'Of course not.'

'What an extraordinary thing to want to know! I call it ghoulish. She has unhealthy tendencies—a relaxation from too much toeing the line, I suppose.'

So Joan was thinking about that too. He also had their mother's end, if not uppermost in his mind, occupying the middle layers of it. At night when he woke it occupied his whole mind. In the blackness of his room all else fell away and he was confronted by the end she had made, an un-forgettable and—after everything else—unforgivable end. He was obliged to put on the light, read a book, walk about on his landing or the next above. But not on the one below, where her room was.

He and Joan had to pass it to get to their own rooms. Going up the stairs they had gone up thousands of times before, they still braced themselves, they still had they knew not what to lose. Was it likely they could go up those stairs any other way yet? Neither bracing nor steeling had ever helped. She had shattered them beyond redemption more than once—oh much more than once! And still was shattering them with the end she had made.

'It's all over.' He spoke it not as a fact but as a comfort noise like 'hush, hush', or 'there, there'.

'I'm glad Helen didn't arrive yesterday evening,' said Joan.

172

GLORY, GLORY ALLELUJAH

They had spent the evening burying empty whisky bottles. Darby had counted over a hundred. They had begun rounding up the bottles the day after she died. What a treasure hunt that had been—with her lying in a tidy mountain on her bed! They found the bottles in drawers, in hatboxes, in suit-cases, behind the bath, under chairs, swaddled in blankets and thrust up the chimney. 'Do you suppose she tried to hide them?' Darby had said. They longed to credit her with some-thing. Once they paused beside her and saw a look of the parrot in her stark repose. Was there anyone else who in her last moments on earth could look like a mountain with the face of a parrot?

Joan stood up and gazed about her challengingly. 'Every-thing is different. We shall feel it soon.'

Now that she was dead, now that she was buried, what was there to wait for? They had only themselves to locate and resurrect and coax back to life.

'I'm beginning to feel it already,' said Joan.

Darby wasn't. Where he was not numb he was going through the motions of the last forty years. If he looked at the ceiling she was up there. 'You can have me above you or you can have God.' They had had her of course, and been damned. If he looked at the door it was to realise that she had hardly needed to use it because she never left them. When she did use it, what an entry, what a manifestation! Not sounding brass or mailed fist, but a huge body creaking and a huger voice. If he looked at Joan, his twin sister, she was born of the same mother in the same hour.

'Will you change the curtains?'

Joan laughed. She seldom smiled and almost never laughed. 'I'll do more, I'll change myself. I'll grow my hair and get new clothes, I may get a fur coat—nothing expensive, beaver lamb— it will do something for me. I'll join clubs, meet people, have friends, go to parties.'

'What sort of clubs?'

'A tennis club, a darts club, a night club. It doesn't matter. I'll travel, I'll become a vegetarian, I'll take lessons, any lessons. I'm free to!'

They stared at each other, the declaration made. Was it too soon? Was it going to be assimilable?

Joan seized a chair and spun it aside. 'Free to climb a mountain, live in a barrel, fly in a balloon, go into a nunnery!' She whirled about, her arms flung wide like an evangelist. 'And so are you, you're free to do anything you like!'

What would he like to do? He would have to think, re-examine all the things he had wanted to do in forty years of life. The handcuffs were off.

'She never stopped us, she never *acted* to stop us.'

'There was no need,' said Joan.

Wanting to fly a kite, long ago, he had stood with the thing in his hands and the wind ready to take it and not been able to move. She was watching and already he had spiked the kite on a thorn-bush and drowned it in the pond. There was no need to move. She said once, 'Do you know what darbies are? They're handcuffs.'

He said, 'I'll go to Bayreuth.'

'You go every year.'

'It's what I want to do.'

Joan's eye was fierce, almost daring him. They were in this together but perhaps she was afraid that that was something he didn't want. He said doubtfully, 'I'll think about that job in Boston.'

'Think, think—let's both have a long think about anything under the sun.'

'Of course I wouldn't go to America and leave you alone.'

'Why not? You have your life and I have mine.'

He looked at her sharply. Gaiety he mistrusted, he could see them foundering if she tried to be gay.

'She had hers,' said Joan, 'in Johannesburg before we were born and if she said it was a good life, depend upon it, it was.'

174

'Good? Leaving aside the moral interpretation, yes.'

Joan went to the window and stood with her back to him. 'I have no further suggestions.'

'I have. The first thing we'll do is get rid of the Green Belt.'

Joan shrugged. 'We only have to let it die.'

'Think so? Those things would do best of all in the sere and yellow. Can't you see it? The hispids a mass of dusty coconut matting and the elephantia rubberendrons mummified for ever and the bones of the reticulata spikata rattling like mad. I tell you I won't have them turning into a lot of carcasses to reproach us with.'

'What will you do?'

'Burn them. I've thought of it many a time.'

'I used to imagine something happening,' said Joan. 'A mysterious blight that would kill them off. I didn't dare contemplate doing anything myself. She was so fond of them.'

'Not fond. There were things she had to have and things she had to be, but ultimately she didn't give a damn. Or that was all she did give—damns. Come and say goodbye to the enemy, it's going to be a happy release for us.'

He opened the door to the conservatory. The air beyond was warm and wet and began at once to load the small hairs inside their noses.

'This is where I felt she was right, I felt that if the point was demonstrable it was demonstrated here. Perhaps I was a bit fanciful, but this place makes me fanciful.'

'What point?'

'About living organisms and there being no need for heart and mind. We'd do better without, in fact we'd have a distinct natural advantage. Like them—' he pointed to the plants, 'and like her.'

Joan raised her eyebrows. 'How long have you had these thoughts?'

'As long as we've been stoking and raking and coming here

175

night and day year in, year out, to check the humidity and temperature, as long as we've weeded and watered and pruned and potted. Since she bawled out our last handyman.'

'Will it give you satisfaction to destroy them?'

'Immense satisfaction.' He stepped on the duckboard between the plants. They sprang up and cascaded down, gripping, twining, stabbing: they hung in the air, leaves like plates and leaves like cogs and gap-toothed leaves as thick as lino and bunches of filaments that crept in the draught. They swelled out of their pots some of them, on goitrous stems or shocked with coarse brown hairs.

'Look, they toil not neither do they spin and Solomon at his worst wasn't arrayed like one of these. You know as well as I do why she kept them. They were a hook, a regular daily hook to hang us on.'

He struck the water-tank with his fist until it boomed and Joan cried, 'Do you have to do that?'

He had to, but they hardly needed the reminder. Hardly. Their mother used to beat on the tank with her stick to summon or deride them. She used the tank like a gong, people heard her travelling great voice from miles away. They used to say – telling Joan and Darby that they had said it – 'There she goes again, she's off!' She stood among her plants banging and shouting and laughing, she was no mother to her son and daughter but she was their island and they could not get away.

'We'll have an *auto-da-fé*, I know how to make these things burn –'

Joan said, 'Piggott's come.'

Darby looked through the glass and there was Piggott in the vegetable patch, pulling up and screwing off radishes.

'So much for your speech of unwelcome.'

'I'll get rid of him!'

Darby stormed out in elation. Here indeed would be a difference, after all they had put up with. Their mother had employed this man against them as she employed everything against them, but she had not needed to pervert Piggott because he was their natural enemy.

'I'll throw him out!' Darby breathed fire, this time Piggott would feel it burn.

'Be careful,' Joan called after him. 'Remember the sort of man he is—'

Darby wasn't likely to overlook that. He had ceased to marvel at Piggott's baseness, he knew that their mother had chosen him with an eye for the harm he could do.

'Look here!' shouted Darby before he was in earshot and Piggott, taking it for a greeting, waved a handful of radish leaves. It was typical. He had dipped for years into their goods, from tintacks to whisky.

'Leave those alone!'

'These?' Piggott opened his palm on two muddy radishes. 'We haven't got many, the birds take them—'

'Birds?'

'Or rabbits or something. And my sister's fond of radishes.'

'They stick in my gullet.' Piggott cleaned the radishes with his thumb and put them in Darby's hand. 'I don't want to deprive you.'

'And get out of our garden.'

Piggott stepped over the radish bed on to the path. He lined up his rubber-booted feet side by side. 'There.'

'Right out!' Darby pointed to the gate. 'And don't come back.'

Piggott held up his thumb and forefinger an inch apart. 'I'll take that much from you for grief, and that much for her—' measuring his arm from elbow to wrist. 'More than that I'll take offence at.'

'It'll be the last thing you'll take from us!'

'Steady, lad.'

Part of his heresy was to credit himself with being a much older and wiser man and to live, when it suited him, like a much younger one. To be called 'lad' by someone only a year or so his senior was insulting to Darby. But it wasn't the insult which went home, it was the gratuitous memory of Piggott's habit of calling their mother 'my love'.

'It's finished, the party's over. Did you think it would last for ever? We did. When we heard you together up in her room we seemed to have been listening to it all our lives. She used to tell us not to worry, she'd sell her stocks and the house, and us too if need be, to pay for the stuff you drank.'

'Sell you?' Piggott laughed, making great play with the muscles of his thick brown neck. 'What a devil!'

'All good things come to an end. Bad things last a little longer but only a little. The tap's turned off, whisky won't flow like water in this house any more, it won't even flow like whisky, there'll be no more drunken debaucheries —'

'Debaucheries my arse,' said Piggott. 'We had a drink together and played cards. That's all.'

'She was an old woman and senile —'

Piggott held his fist before Darby's nose. 'If someone else had said that I'd knock him down. Your mother wouldn't have been senile if she'd lived to a hundred. She loved life and she had a mind like a whip.'

'And that's how she used it,' said Joan, coming to Darby's side.

When Piggott had greeted Liza he used to pull off his hat with a sweeping gesture and clap it to his left breast, laughing as he did so. Those two started to laugh as soon as they saw each other.

To Joan, now, he tugged briefly at the brim.

'Why didn't you go away if it didn't suit you?'

'Why should we? This is our home. And it was our duty to look after her.'

'You look after her?' Piggott was a tall man, he put his hands on his knees and stooped to peer into their faces. 'What's with you two? She looked after herself. She managed her affairs and yours as well and advised me on mine. She was the most sufficient person, man or woman, I ever met or ever shall meet. She built up fifty thousand pounds worth of solid stock out of the rubbish your old man left her. And she left you property worth as much again if you handle it right.'

'You've been spying,' cried Darby. 'Even *she* had enough common decency not to discuss our private affairs with you.'

'You wouldn't promise me one thing, would you? If you're ever disposed to sell any of your hereditament, let me know first? I might be able to stop you making a mistake. It's easily done if you don't know the property market and she and I went into it pretty thoroughly.'

'What do you think we are? Do you think we'll tie ourselves to you as we were tied to her?' Darby turned to Joan. 'He does! He thinks we'll creep under his thumb, he thinks Liberty Hall's still open—'

'Shush, lad.' Piggott sighed. 'I wanted to help you.'

'Why?' asked Joan.

'Search me. It wouldn't break her heart if you balled things up, she half expected that, but I suppose it might take the skin off my nose after all the work we put in.'

'Work! You've never worked in your life. You were drinking and brawling night and day—'

'We didn't brawl, lad, we used to sing sometimes. Believe it or not, we found something to sing about.'

'You used this house as a tavern and made our name a byword. People think my sister and I are tarred with your brush—'

'Embarrassed are you? You needn't be. Gossip's not what it used to be, people have a lot on their minds nowadays and they don't notice so much.'

'You made sure they noticed,' said Joan. 'You destroyed us and you enjoyed doing it. Part of your sickness is to destroy what you don't understand.'

Piggott looked thoughtful. 'We do that just by trying to understand. Do a breakdown on anything and what are you left with? Parts, not the whole. Certainly I don't understand you two, certainly I've tried. Perhaps it's a mistake to think you're interchangeable, you being twins. What I ought to settle first is are you halves or wholes?'

A robust roar erupted out of his chest and he put his hand over his mouth. 'Gassy things, radishes. Mind you, she wanted to shield you. She told me you'd never been born. "I'll have to take them with me. Remember," she said to me, "there'll be three of us buried when they put me under". Those were her words.'

'What did she mean?' asked Joan.

'I don't know what you're talking about and I don't have to!' Darby was observing, with rage and relief, that Piggott had not bothered to put on a black tie and show ordinary decency or respect, he still wore his shirt open to the waist like a gipsy and was careful to keep his shoulders back so that the shirt would gap and reveal the hair on his chest.

'This is our house now and it'll be run decently and respectably—'

'I don't suppose I'll be coming here any more. There's nothing to come for. Does that sound ungracious?' Piggott turned to Joan. 'It's not meant to.'

'You mean what you say,' said Darby, 'and well we know it. The supply of free liquor's run dry and the free meals and there's no chance of getting any more money out of her.'

'Money?'

'You could always get that, couldn't you? I don't know how much you've had and don't want to, but you've cheated her for years.'

Piggott said softly, 'Hush up, lad. I didn't cheat and she was a better card player than me and we didn't play for money.'

'You got it at other games then,' said Joan.

She and Piggott stared at each other and something passed between them, bypassing Darby. He had an incidental feeling as if whatever it was was the heart of the matter and other considerations were being used to cover up the real thing which was even less presentable, wasn't presentable at all.

'This once I'll tell you it's not true. I'm just telling you quietly,' said Piggott, 'because you don't know me. Why should you know me? But don't ever say it again because you should know her a little, you really should know her enough never to say that.'

Joan was still staring. Piggott was smiling and Darby moved away, he didn't care to be near anything that was likely to explode.

'It was thoroughly unhealthy,' said Joan.

'Oh, I don't think so. We went out in the fresh air whenever she felt inclined.'

'You know what I mean. A man like you—' Joan probably coloured, but on her it would only amount to a darkening of the brown of her skin, 'unmarried—and she was an old woman—'

'I know what you mean, I know what you both mean.' Piggott looked from Joan to Darby. 'Is it possible to be cuckolded by your own mother?' and burst out laughing.

They watched him walk along the path through the vegetable patch. He paused to pull up a handful of mint.

'Leave that alone!' Darby sounded absurd even to himself.

Piggott chafed the leaves in his palms and sniffed them before he took off his hat in farewell.

'I'd have married her if she'd have taken me.'

They caught a strong whiff of the crushed mint and Joan supposed that now she would be obliged to think of him whenever she smelt it. As if there weren't enough associations! The place was cocooned, so was she, so was Darby, in the thing between Piggott and their mother. What right had *that* to smell of fresh mint?

'I was ready to knock him down.' Darby caressed his knuckles. 'It's what I've wanted to do for years.'

'He'd have let you I expect if you'd told him it was for her sake.'

'What do you mean?'

'Oh why don't we shut up!' cried Joan. 'Asking what we mean! You know as well as I do!'

'No I don't. And nor do you and I should think we've had enough snide remarks from him. We knew he was a black-guard and he's confirmed it out of his own mouth. Suppose he'd persuaded her to marry him?'

Joan had already supposed and found it horrifying. She hadn't wanted to think about it, had not planned to except as a waking nightmare.

'We'd have been dispossessed, left penniless.'

'She could have left him everything anyway.'

'If she'd married him I doubt if we could have broken the will. But she kept her head, thank God.' Darby grunted. 'She probably enjoyed that too.'

'Enjoyed what?'

'It was something, wasn't it, at her age, to turn a man down?'

'And it would be at my age, wouldn't it? Always supposing I was asked. Oh, I take your meaning!'

Darby opened his mouth and shut it again. 'Of course she wouldn't enjoy it as much as having him for a husband. Her husband! Our stepfather!'

Joan turned and ran.

There was no smell of mint in the conservatory, thank heaven. She was up against a simple tyranny there. In some-thing like gratitude she began to fill the containers to water the plants.

It was true that women were fools. God made them so for His good reasons and there was no more shame in it than in a monkey's being given a tail.

They had attended to the plants at this time every day and sometimes Mother came to supervise. Joan had never ceased to be destroyed, even after a lifetime — even now at the thought. She used to avert her eyes, going from plant to plant, she hardly looked at her mother. It was the best she could do: she had to listen, she had to feel but she need not look.

'What are you doing?' Darby came and took the can out of her hand. 'We're going to burn them.'

'Now?'

'Now!'

He began to knock the plants to the floor. The bigger ones he seized by the stems as if they were people he was seizing by the throat. There was a crash of breaking pots and the smell of the place intensified almost unbearably.

Soil spilled over Joan's feet. All round her the pendulous, the woody, the umbelliferous, the glabrous, the corneous, the hairy, the spiculate, came crashing down. Their ruins mounted to her knees and she watched as she had when they were children and Darby tried some tricky boy's thing which it was important to him to accomplish.

She did not move as the falling leaves buffeted her. Years ago, when he had achieved whatever he was trying to achieve, or at least had shown that it wasn't dangerous or especially unpleasant, she used to try it too. But not this, this wasn't the way.

'I don't know why you want to do it.'

He stopped with an *encephalaratos horridens* held high and looked at her. 'Have you forgotten already?'

'Forgotten? I'll never live that long. I don't even need to remember yet!'

'Nor do I.' Darby threw the potted palm at the water-tank. 'And I'm not going to leave these to remind me to forget.'

'They won't burn, they're too green.'

'They will, with wood shavings and paraffin to help.'

183

'They look like crashed birds,' said Joan.

Darby kicked at the broken-winged green. 'Did you think that if we kept these and went on watering and feeding them and warming them they'd turn into plants? Something pleasurable that we could have for fun? To show our friends? When we get friends?'

'They've never done us any harm.'

'Everything's done us harm. We're the most harmed people alive. If you won't help me I'll do it myself. I'm going to burn the lot.'

He began to carry armfuls of plants into the garden and after a moment Joan stooped and gathered up those at her feet. A thorn pierced her finger and she thought again that this wasn't the way.

She glanced up at the sky as she carried out her load. It would soon be dark and the clouds were packing in across the Weald. She hoped—oh she did hope!—that this was the way for Darby, anyway for Darby, and that it wouldn't rain.

'Perhaps we should do it tomorrow.'

He looked at her over his armful of leaves. He had a scratch on one cheek and his black tie was cocked sideways.

'I'll be back at school tomorrow.'

After that they worked in silence and urgency, carrying out the plants and heaping them with layers of wood shavings and paraffin-soaked paper. He had chosen a place in sight of the house. 'Here,' he said, and they looked up at her window where she used to stand to watch them go when they were going anywhere, or just to see what she called 'the colour of the day'. In the summer she leaned on the sill, her chin in her hands. Joan, coming back from the village, would see her red hair shouting against the dark walls of the house.

When there were no more broken stems and floundering leaves to carry out and the glass walls of the conservatory were like a tank emptied of its fish, Darby put his hand on her shoulder and brought her to the edge of the pyre. And

184

Joan uttered fervently for them both, 'I hope we're doing the right thing!'

Darby struck a match. The fire, sprightly at first, grew languid as it reached the green leaves.

'It's not going to burn!' cried Joan, dismayed.

He upended the paraffin can and the flames leapt with a smack. They transformed the heap into liquid brass, flowing to its apex as smoothly as the solid coil of a machine.

'When the sap dries out it'll burn like any other bonfire.'

Would it? They both knew that that would not do, there must be nothing average about this fire. Joan watched with fierce anxiety. She was willing it not to lose heart, not to eat up daintily, not to drop to a smoulder or a smother, not to burn like any other bonfire.

'I should have done this years ago,' said Darby.

The brass was falling into caves, indigo and violet, and Joan wondered which was making the midnight holes — the fibrous or the oily plants? Or the hormones she had fed them? Or the jungle where they should have been? Or what they had been used for?

'I've so often thought about this — Don't let that take the heart out of the doing of it!' cried Darby, to himself or to the fire. He took a stick and lifted the pile to let the air under each corner.

'What did she mean about taking us with her?'

'She didn't say that. She wouldn't. Can you hear her?'

'Yes,' said Joan.

'Well I can't. She wasn't morbid and she never would talk about dying, even when she knew she was. Remember what happened when we tried to prepare her?'

Joan shuddered. It had been the last act. A Very Reverend gentleman had received half a bottle of whisky over his cloth. They hadn't realised that she still had half a bottle of whisky and less than a moment to live — she used both against her children. As the clergyman came to her bedside she dragged

185

the bottle from under the blankets and threw it at him. She died doing it but she did it well. He was hit on the temple and his coat and vest were soaked by the spirit. 'Miss Brown!' he cried—he blamed Joan—'I shall never obliterate the smell!'

Darby lifted something blackened and flaccid on his stick. It was the *encephalaratos horridens*.

'Piggott just said it to frighten you.'

Joan found this notion of what would frighten her ridiculous, and offensive, coming from Piggott. Of course he didn't know her, he judged her as a man like that would judge, by crude and material standards. But she knew more than enough of him. His offence was enormous and she held it against the whole world.

'A man like that is out to make trouble.'

A man like the nights and days he had spent in this house, like the noises and the silences from that room, like 'my love' to an old woman.

'Mother was a whore,' said Joan.

Darby turned. He was bright and blank from bending over the fire, as bright and blank as the thickness of glass. His cheeks were rosy and Joan was confronted by his face, untouched and untouchable as she had not seen it since his schoolboy days.

'They're going to burn!'

They were. Liza Brown's bit of Africa was going up in flame. The brass flame had bred into a score, forked and joyous. They fattened on the hairy stems and made black blubber of the pan-shaped leaves. Joan watched the fronds of a palm fire and drop off one by one.

'It's the beginning!' cried Darby. 'If this is done in the green tree what shall be done in the dry?'

Was he shocked? As a very young man he was shocked to tears. Joan remembered the drops standing on his skin and their mother's amusement. He had always amused her, once she had said: 'He's not anyone's fool, he's mine'.

He was pouring the last of the paraffin on the flames. They fused and leapt up like a genie and he stood staring with their light all over his face. Then he seized Joan's hand and swung it above their heads in a winner's gesture.

'It's what we are that matters—what we're going to be!'

'What are we going to be?'

'Free!'

He pulled her with him into a rocking caper. She resisted at first and then, more in faith than madness, ran with him. Hand in hand they circled the fire. Darby was shouting, 'Glory, glory!' and the flames capered with them, ragged and artful. The dry wood went off with shrill cracks like a children's war and the green stuff sang. At the centre the bones of the plants held up white and pure before melting into ash.

The heat was fierce, so was the smoke. Joan, beginning to be breathless, swallowed it whole. She stumbled and the flames flattened for her like a tiger for a spring. Darby pulled her back.

'It was the smoke, it smells so queer—'

Darby crushed the sparks out of her hair. 'What do you expect? It's not an ordinary bonfire, we're not burning rubbish.'

'What are we burning?'

'You ask that?'

He did and didn't look like Darby. His hair stood on end, his face was sweaty and she was asking herself, was this all? Darby with a dirty face wasn't going to be enough.

'Knowing what those things did to us? Tending and feeding them, washing and dressing them, keeping them warm, keeping them wet? Every day of our lives? I'm burning those hairy weeds because she made me feel they were better than I am.' He shook her by the shoulders, none too gently. 'You've got plenty to burn—burn it!'

The fire was at its height, they saw the garden and each other shaken out like flags against the dark. Behind them was the house—but the house was her banner. It was full of her, it staked her on the ground, in the air, under the sun. They two were campers out.

'This is the best bonfire we've ever had!' cried Darby.

'It's ours,' said Joan, 'something we can call our own.'

Another Thing

DILYS CRAIG and Gwen Beaumont (Gwen Windsor that was) had always been friends. They agreed, without sentiment, that the time before they met was negligible. It had served merely to identify them: Dilys was the practical one, the activator, Gwen the leave-it-to-chancer. At their very first encounter Dilys had to warn Gwen that her bean-bag was leaking. Dilys retrieved the spilled beans and gave them to Gwen who squeezed them back through the hole. It was Dilys who pointed out that she was thereby making the hole bigger and that if they were going to have to pick up after her bag they would have no time to play with it.

Gwen married, Dilys did not. It was a joke between them that she could not find a man good enough. As a matter of fact it was true because in a husband she would want the best of herself and no more.

Gwen told her that was why she had no luck. 'You're asking the impossible.' Gwen knew what she was talking about, she had twice married, divorced one husband and outlived the other.

Looking back on their lives they saw no cause for regret. If it were all to do again they would not wish to change anything. Not even her first marriage, Gwen said. She had learned a lot from it, a 'crash course in living' she called it.

'But for Tony I'd never have been ready for Arnold. He would have been way over my head and someone else would have got him. There's nothing like a romantic marriage to teach a girl sense.'

Dilys, who had not needed teaching, agreed that Gwen had done well. Mistakes came naturally to her but she learned by them and now could afford the little indiscretions she enjoyed. At fifty-five she had a house, a car and a generous fixed income. 'I don't know what from,' she told Dilys, 'and don't care. It's safe. Arnold never monkeyed with money.'

Dilys too was well provided for and knew exactly what with because she did it herself. She much preferred to. It was her living in more than the one material way. She had a small hotel in West Kensington, quiet, Palm Courtish and unpermissive. People remembered it if not with affection with relief, and came back because they did not feel conned there, did not sense, as in other hotels, a secret life which guests were incidental to but would surely be financing. Dilys had furnished it in a style distilled by hotels all over the Home Counties. Vice, it was felt, would be a sort mentionable in front of the Heals wardrobes. Dilys's candour informed the place, so also did her good sense, which some people found themselves unequal to.

Gwen, newly widowed, was coming to stay. 'You will take me out of myself,' she wrote, and Dilys, knowing that it would need a bulldozer to do that, hoped that Gwen wasn't finding her loss too hard to bear.

She more than decently concealed it. When she descended from the taxi in West Kensington she was the same old charmer. The air filled with her soft little cries. Like doves, thought Dilys, she sounds like a cote of doves. But Gwen was as fond of a fight as anyone.

'Darling!' she cried from the pavement, seeing Dilys on the inside of the swing doors. 'Darling evergreen Dilly!' as they met, clung and kissed in the foyer. 'You don't look a day over seven!' She often proclaimed the absurd, relieving people of the bother of wondering if she meant it and leaving them room to supply the truth for themselves somewhere in between. 'I've such reams to tell you!'

Indeed she had, and was happy telling it. Dilys was content to hear. She knew all Gwen's family, their quiddities and powers were a rich vein of interest in her life. And Gwen herself, new to the role of widow but filling it — as she filled all wants, felt or unfelt, all hiatuses and lacks — as to the manner born, like the good friend she was occasionally paused to exclaim, 'That's enough about me, I want to hear about you.'

There wasn't much to tell about Dilys. She kept life on an even keel, if anything went wrong she put it right without fuss. What happened to Dilys was mostly programmed, by Dilys herself, by government departments and by trades unions. For human events — those she cared to have — she relied on other people. Her news was about the hotel and the hotel guests. Gwen asked after the residents and the regulars.

'Is Miss Corelli-Brown still here? And the Punsetts? What colour's her hair now?'

'Miss Corelli-Brown's hair is brown.'

'Now, Dilly, you well know I'm not asking about her. She'll always be as God made her. But if Mrs. Punsett's gone magenta again I shall tell her about a Swiss preparation I've discovered.' Her black clothes suited Gwen. White did too. She had the sort of colouring which triumphs over extremes, benefited by them in fact. 'Does the Commissar still come for Wimbledon? Heavens, what a flagpole! I wonder, does he fly the Union Jack or the Red Flag?'

'I don't care so long as he pays his bill.'

'Do you know what I think? I think you're the reason he comes. He fancies you. The tennis is just an excuse.'

'What nonsense.'

'I have always thought so,' said Gwen. 'Don't underestimate yourself, Dilly. You're very personable and you've got a pretty little figure in the bank.'

'One swallow doesn't make a summer.'

They both laughed, then Gwen sighed and took Dilys's

hand. 'You've missed something by not marrying and having a family.'

'If I've missed one thing I've had another.'

'I don't like to think of you being alone.'

Dilys said gently, 'But you're alone now,' and they looked at each other in recognition.

'I suppose I am. Arnold's gone and the children are married.' Gwen's eyes filled. 'Oh, Dilly, I don't want to be!'

'Then stay here with me. Stay as long as you like. For good if you like.'

Both felt that it would be for all possible good and for the ultimate best. Here they were, both solitary, and here was Dilys with room to spare and as Gwen said, it was such joy for her not to be harassed with running a house. She felt free as air. And they were such friends. Friends for life. They could never be alone while they had each other.

Dilys always enjoyed having Gwen around. There was no overlooking her presence, she didn't need to be evident in flesh or property to make it felt. She had not changed since beanbag days, she still left small possessions in her wake and Dilys found it warming to pick up after her.

She gave her one of the nicest rooms in the hotel. On windy days it was possible to see the tops of the trees tossing in the Park. But Gwen was seldom in her room. She spent a lot of time in the lounge, holding a little court there.

Perhaps because she lived for the moment and never doubted that the moment was for ever people tended to gravitate to her. Here was someone to listen. Dipping into Gwen's pocket of time relieved and comforted people: as Miss Corelli-Brown wistfully put it—'Like a tiny holiday'.

Dilys smiled at that. But she knew the feeling. Sometimes in the evenings she took an hour of Gwen's time for herself. They sat in Dilys's room which overlooked the well of the hotel where the kitchens were. The clatter of dishes and the voices of the night staff amused Gwen.

'Do they realise how audible they are from up here?'

'I've told them often enough. But of course they can't close the windows, it gets too hot in the kitchen.'

'At least you're in touch. If you want to know what they're thinking you can come up and listen.'

'Oh I know that soon enough. It's what they're doing, and not doing that concerns me.'

'Why don't you give yourself a nice room at the front?'

'Because I'd lose money. And what would be the point of having a good room empty all day? When you're not here I spend my evenings downstairs in the office. Or at the desk.'

When the evening receptionist failed to turn up Dilys had to take over until the night porter came at nine.

'Now that's something I could do,' said Gwen. 'You work yourself too hard, Dilly. Let me help.'

'It would be unethical. You're here as a guest.'

But Gwen said damn ethics she was here as Dilys's friend, her best friend, and if they were going to be together they must give and take. So, with some misgiving—the reception desk ensured encounters which were best kept brief and not social, not in the foyer, a rather small foyer that looked like standing-room only if there were more than six people in it—Dilys agreed, trusting that the need wouldn't often arise.

Of course it soon did: the evening clerk gave notice and the employment agency sent no one suitable in her place. Gwen insisted on relieving while Dilys had her dinner and Dilys was explaining the working of the switchboard to her when the American girl arrived.

Gwen said she would have known her by her clothes, they were so English and so classic that only an American would wear them all at once. And her looks, Gwen said, identified her as from one of those fifth or sixth generation Washington families of bankers or lawyers.

Dilys saw a pale gangling girl with straight hair cut in a fringe, wearing a belted camel coat and a round hat and carrying one small suitcase. She spoke only to ask for a room, to all questions about her requirements she shook her head or nodded. She registered as 'Augusta Smith, Tacoma'.

'Tacoma in Washington State?' Gwen asked her.

Then she did say one thing. She said, 'Does it matter?' and they were surprised by the desolation in her voice.

'Room twenty,' Dilys told her, 'on the second floor. I hope you'll be comfortable.'

The girl followed the porter upstairs. She tramped up, having largish feet which she was too tired or too indifferent to do more than propel herself with.

'What do you make of that?' said Gwen.

'I make it a single room and breakfast, no morning tea. Bath, if she takes it, will be extra.'

'You know that's not what I mean. I wonder who she is.'

'Augusta Smith.'

'Augusta—yes. Smith, no. Obviously it's not her real name.'

'Lots of people *are* named Smith.'

'Not Americans. It's not an American alias. They'd call themselves Crumpacker. And did you notice there were no labels on her case?'

'Perhaps this is the first time she's used it.'

'Isn't it a long way from Tacoma, with just one little bag?'

Dilys smiled. 'As Miss Smith herself said, "Does it matter?" '

But Gwen's estimate of what was material and what was immaterial differed radically from Dilys's. And they could both be right. Gwen, after all, was not in the hotel business though she tried hard to understand it for Dilys's sake. Gwen was just a very human being—which was not to say merely, but simply, without circumspection. Luckily she could afford to be. The complexities of earning a living would have spoiled her and by now she was totally unfitted for it. She hadn't even got the priorities right—but for this Dilys loved her. She could indulge Gwen, it was Gwen's indulgences she objected to when they were at her own expense. Like Mrs. Punsett's night-cap.

'Figuratively speaking', she would have said, because she wasn't counting the cost of a glass of milk. It was the principle. She did not wish to be God, but dispensations should come or not come from her. Gwen, just by being Gwen, put her at a disadvantage and being deeply bothered, all Dilys could express was botheration.

It was no wonder that the Punsetts had latched on to Gwen. General Punsett was a blank silent man, stunned by some old battle long ago. His days and his wife's were passed strictly within the hotel timetable, they had no other laws and no other engagements. Gwen came as a revelation. Even to the General something was revealed: he leaned perceptibly towards her from his dark corner in the hotel lounge. And Mrs. Punsett began to twitter just as she did when she first came to the hotel. She sounded like a very small bird, a Jenny Wren, thawing out.

'Why didn't she ask me?' said Dilys. 'There are people here who are paid to serve her. She's paying them.'

'Do you know what she said? She said, "It's like being in my own home to have a glass of hot milk at night. We've never had a home," she said, "the General doesn't care for domesticity".'

'She only needed to order milk and she'd have had it taken to her every night.'

'She doesn't want it every night, she wants it now and then when she's feeling low. Dilly, it isn't bothering the night staff or taking them from their work. It was my idea, I go to the kitchen and warm some milk for her—'

'Slippers too?'

Gwen laughed. 'She doesn't wear slippers, the General won't allow it. Dilly, you wouldn't believe such a little thing would be such a luxury for her. Oh, of course we're paying for the milk, this is the third time she's had it, that's three glasses we owe for.'

'Why didn't she ask me?'

'Would you believe it, the silly old darling's a bit afraid of you.'

Dilys turned and walked away. One of the chambermaids was beckoning to her and Gwen need not notice how upset she was. It was absurd, over such a trifle.

Gwen obviously didn't see the crux of the incident. She was happy with the promise to pay for Mrs. Punsett's milk, a promise she devotedly kept. Dilys found sixpences on the desk in her office or by her plate at the table she and Gwen shared. Gwen made it their little joke but she was adamant about Dilys's taking the money.

'You must.' Laughing, she would fold Dilys's fingers over the coin. 'For the principle!'

Dilys, the words taken out of her mouth, was obliged to smile too, recognising the teeny tiny grit between them. Of course it was there. Now that she came to think of it—perhaps Gwen was thinking of it too—they were essentially diverse. The attraction of opposites, people said of their friendship. And every now and then they got beyond the friendship, beyond the attraction to the oppositeness.

But it was hard on Dilys to be taken at the face-value of sixpence. Why did the absurd matter of Mrs. Punsett's milk have intimations about herself and Gwen and human relationships? The more she thought about it the more she might— without profit obviously, and probably without conclusion. She tried to dismiss it from her mind and accept the sixpences as Gwen's little nonsense.

Gwen, if she also felt their dichotomy, was not put out by it. She had been known to say, 'Dilys and I are chalk and cheese', but had never by one jot adapted her acts or outlook to Dilys's. This was not intransigence so much as happiness with her own point of view.

She began conjecturing about the American. 'That girl isn't happy.'

'Is she not?'

'Don't you notice, Dilly? She walks about like a ghost.'

'A substantial ghost. She has the room above mine and I hear her tramping up and down half the night.'

'There you are, there's something wrong.'

'If there is it's her affair.'

Gwen, although she always said she could take a hint, couldn't. 'At her age there's only one thing to go wrong.'

'At ours, thank God, we do have a choice.'

Gwen giggled. 'Do you remember that priest we were so crazy about? We used to wait for him and sit beside him on the tram. I pretended to trip and he caught me in his arms. We were going to turn Catholic, you said all the consummation you ever wanted was to have him give you the sacrament. It wasn't though, was it?'

'You know very well it wasn't.'

They both laughed. 'If you weren't such a perfectionist,' said Gwen, 'you'd have made some man very happy.'

They were having their late dinner together and the American was still at her table by the window. People liked the window seats because they could look into the street where there was always something going on and at night the pleasant orange lamps were lit among the trees. Augusta Smith did not give it a second glance. Had she given it a first? She hunched unbecomingly, scoring the tablecloth with the point of her knife.

'I'll put it on her bill,' said Dilys, 'if she makes so much as one cut. And she almost certainly will because what passes for linen nowadays is only glazed cotton.'

'Is that brandy she's drinking?'

'She's of age.'

'A girl like that shouldn't be knocking it back as if it was water!'

'I agree. It's a three-star brandy.'

'How would you feel if she were your daughter?'

'If she were drinking on the house I'd feel watchful.'

Augusta Smith stood up. She moved carefully across the room, resting the tips of her fingers wherever she could. Gwen smiled at her as she drew near and asked how she was liking London.

'London?' She poised herself with two fingers splayed on their table, seeming intent on keeping something more than her balance.

'I expect you've seen it all. Far more than we have—'

'I haven't noticed.'

'You've been to the palaces and the parks and the towers— London's and the Post Office's?'

'No.'

'But what are your friends about? Why don't they take you to see the sights?'

'I don't have friends.'

She was moving away with a gesture both desperate and dismissive.

'My dear!' Augusta Smith did not look round and Gwen was left saying, 'Well I never!'

'Oh come,' said Dilys, 'it does happen occasionally—she's certainly not an outgoing girl.'

'How wrong can you be? With all your opportunities for learning about people! That girl is completely and utterly outgoing but her effluent's blocked.'

The hotel was often full that winter and Dilys had a lot of staff trouble. She was kept busy just maintaining the daily norm—what people paid for when they came in out of the cold. Gwen was a great help. Attention to detail was not her strong point, but public relations was, and guests who worried about locking their doors at night, or whether the chambermaid was honest, or why their letters didn't arrive, turned to Gwen. If Gwen made them feel more comfortable or better catered for, Dilys was glad. She just didn't have the time.

The staff knew it. 'Miss Craig hasn't time to listen,' they

said, 'Mrs. Beaumont has', and the night porter who was old-fashioned enough to use the word, added, 'She's a lady.' Dilys accepted the distinction as being one of time. A woman who had to keep herself had precious little for anything else: a woman who was kept, respectably or otherwise, had time to be a lady if she was that way disposed. Gwen, impractical, tender, almost silly-hearted, was a natural.

She was a mine of secondary and tertiary information. Dilys could rely on her for answers to such unimportant questions as why was the cook rushing to get away. Gwen could tell her because it was Cook's son's birthday, or because Cook's husband was taking Cook to see the Crazy Gang. Useless facts which did not change the shape of the day, but filled it out. Even such unpleasant ones as what was in the madly scrawled envelopes which came for the Company Director from Tiverton did that.

But when a guest referred to the 'Manageress' and her promise to find him a quieter room, Dilys told Gwen: 'He said, "Mrs. Beaumont was kind enough to say that she would arrange everything for me".'

'What a joke!' cried Gwen. 'Wherever did he get that idea?'

' "Mrs. Beaumont is always so very kind", he said.'

'About me being the manageress I mean?'

'It was a natural mistake, but awkward to explain.'

'Are you angry, Dilly?'

'You didn't promise him, did you?'

'Of course not. All I did was promise to look into it. He's right over the kitchen you know, and he was telling me that he was a Battle of Britain pilot and if he doesn't get some sleep before midnight—'

'I can't give him another room, there's none free.'

'Heavens, he'd have more than the noise of the washing-up to grouse about if I was managing this place.'

They laughed. They knew it was true and they had always

been able to laugh at each other. To prove it Gwen squeezed Dilys's hand. 'Let them think what they like, Dilly darling. I promise not to ask to be paid.'

There was certainly a different atmosphere in the hotel – or was there just more of it? Dilys recognised it as a family feeling. She was a little out of her depth, she hadn't been part of a family for years.

It was cosier, the guests not only talked to Gwen, they talked to each other. Things were not as clear-cut as they used to be, people raised little mountains: Dilys noticed afresh how people did that with encouragement – and without. In fact they did it unless they were prevented. Listening to them she wondered, idly for her, whether there would have been less or more history if people had always just done what they were going to do.

Augusta Smith was not absorbed into the cosiness. She hunched her shoulders like the wings of a sick bird and scarcely spoke. She, at least, just did what she was going to do.

What that was nobody knew. She went out occasionally for an hour. The rest of the time she stayed in her room. At meals she drank brandy and pushed her food about on her plate. Once, a letter came for her. Gwen, who was sorting the mail, held up the envelope.

'It's a man's hand. Didn't I say so?'

'I don't think you did.'

'I said she was involved with a man. Look, he's put on a fourpenny stamp!'

'Well?'

'When a girl becomes second-class mail to a man she might as well give up.'

'Perhaps he didn't have a penny.' But that would just have been history, thought Dilys.

'I saw her yesterday in the square. She ran into a telephone box – practically erupted into it – dialled a number and erupted out. There wasn't even time to connect her.'

'Perhaps she didn't have sixpence.' Dilys took the letter which had crossed mountains between the reception-desk and Miss Smith's pigeonhole.

'That reminds me,' said Gwen, 'Mrs. Punsett had milk last night.'

Dilys did not discover how Gwen overcame Augusta Smith's resistance. Perhaps suddenly there was none, perhaps the letter overcame it and Gwen moved in. Of course the girl didn't stand a chance, she was under pressure, the pressure kept her together, it only had to vary a degree one way or the other and she flew apart.

When it happened Dilys was amused and a little vexed. She loved Gwen, there was really no one but Gwen to love, and of course she wanted everything for her. Everything except Augusta Smith, which was curious because Augusta herself mattered not in the least to Dilys. Simply she would have preferred one sizeable failure for Gwen because it wasn't good for Gwen, or anyone, to have all her own way.

'It's worse than I expected,' said Gwen. 'He's married, of course, and he's a bishop or a bonze or something in one of these rich new religions. If he puts a foot wrong he'll be excommunicated and lose his job.'

'Who?' Dilys knew very well, she asked because she was irritated that she knew without having been told.

'Augusta's seducer. The poor child's as unhappy as—as the day is long, and that's a fact. She met him at some conference in New York. They fell passionately in love and the little fool followed him home.'

'Fool indeed.'

'Her parents don't know where she is. They must be out of their minds with worry. And of course he's said it's all over, he can't risk divorce, so there's no future for them.'

'I'm sorry for her. But she'll get over it.'

'She keeps saying she wants to die.'

'Not in my hotel.'

'Oh, Dilly, you talk as if she's a dog that might mess on the carpet! What are we going to do?'

'I shan't do anything. The girl's of age and so long as she pays her bill there's nothing I can do.'

'I keep thinking how I'd feel if it were my Celia alone and friendless and desperately miserable—'

'She is not your Celia,' Dilys said sharply, 'and this is not a family circle, this is a business. People pay me to do what they won't or can't do for themselves. I care to a point, I am not paid to care beyond it.'

'Dilly, you do care about other things besides money.' Tears came to Gwen's eyes. 'You're not to make me think you don't!'

Sometimes Dilys wanted to wring Gwen's neck. That was inevitable in a good friendship when people were able and encouraged to be themselves.

'If I walked into the bosom of your family and tried to run you all as a business you'd object. I object to your running my business as a family.'

'I wouldn't dream of running your business! I'm not clever enough. Arnold said I had the brain of a flea and the heart of a bus. People matter terribly to me—they matter to you too, I know they do!'

'But not terribly, not these people. They're hotel guests, they get what they pay for and I try to give good value. That's all.'

'I'm a hotel guest too,' Gwen said wistfully.

Dilys understood that she was also being tactical. She was stating, and claiming, her right to do as she pleased.

'I've asked Augusta to come and sit with us for supper tonight. You don't mind, do you, Dilly? Just to cheer her up a little?'

There was an ideal between giving and not giving which Dilys tried to achieve. It was the discretionary standard she set herself and she believed that success in business depended on how closely she kept to it.

'Of course I don't mind.'

'It's not good for her to be so much alone.'

Now that should have come from God or from the family doctor. It accepted responsibility for Augusta Smith: cheering her up was one thing, doing her good was another.

'But please don't let's make it a habit. I should say—' Dilys crisped the words—'don't expect me to make it a habit.'

'Of course not, darling. I'm much too fond of our own company.'

Augusta Smith was probably as keen to join them as Dilys was to have her. But then Augusta was in an emotionally exhausted state. She was like an empty banana skin—long empty.

When she came into the dining-room that evening Dilys was startled at the deterioration in her. During the last two days she had used herself up, all that remained was a series of functions and it was natural to wonder, without wishing her harm, why they continued to operate. Certainly not for her benefit because it would have been humane simply to let her cease. To all individual intents and personal purposes, she had.

'Here we are, dear.' Gwen brought her to a chair, settled her in it, making comfort noises. 'This will be a nice change for us, Dilly, won't it?'

'Good evening, Miss Smith.'

Dilys was debating at that moment what impact Augusta Smith could have made on the high priest of the new religion. It was hard to imagine her rousing even a sleeping dog. But youth was resilient. It was also, Dilys thought, arousing *per se*.

'We have a delicious menu tonight,' said Gwen. 'Chicken risotto and Diplomat pudding.'

'It's Mrs. Webb's night off,' said Dilys.

'What will you start with, Augusta? Grapefruit, soup, or Salad Niçoise?'

'Brandy.'

203

'My dear, do you think you should? It's so alcoholic. Dilly and I sometimes have a little wine with our meal, Hock or Graves—'

'We'll have a bottle of white Burgundy tonight.'

'That will be lovely, Dilly. Wine's so civilised. I think they should have stopped at wine, there was really no need to invent spirits—'

'Brandy,' said Augusta Smith.

'It is, of course, derived from the grape.' Dilys beckoned the waiter. 'Bring us a bottle of the 1967 Chablis. You like a fairly dry wine, Miss Smith?'

'I prefer brandy.'

'My dear, why not wait until after the meal? With black coffee, perhaps?'

'Now.'

Dilys shrugged. 'With water it's a good aperitif.'

So the brandy was brought. Augusta splashed out a generous measure, drank and immediately poured another which she sipped as hungrily as if she were tempted to eat the glass.

Gwen said, 'I was telling Augusta that she should see more of London. It seems a pity not to look around while she's here. So much of it will soon be past history. Do you know, she hasn't even been on a bus?'

'What are your plans, Miss Smith?'

Obviously she had none. In her situation she did not plan, she waited for the wind and the rain or for something to stop. Would she know when it happened? Had it happened already, was she simply keeping going on her own momentum?

'How long are you staying in London?'

'She must come with me to Stratford,' said Gwen. 'She'd never forgive herself, Dilly, if she went home without seeing it. It would be like us going to New York and not seeing Washington Square.'

Augusta Smith raised her heavy head and looked at Dilys. 'Do you want my room?'

'You can stay as long as you like. Can't she, Dilly?' Gwen leaned across and lightly held the wrist of the fingers that were round the brandy bottle. 'Now is the time to forget and now is the place to begin.'

'I shall never go home again.'

'What nonsense! Hooey! Isn't that what you call it? This isn't the end of the world.' Gwen laughed. 'The times we thought it was! When we were young—Didn't we, Dilly?'

'I can't say I've ever had that impression.'

'Be honest! There was Mr. Hartsilver—'

'Schoolgirl foolishness.'

'Isn't that what I'm saying? Of course you're not a schoolgirl, Augusta, but these things happen to all of us and we live to smile at them.'

'Mrs. Beaumont has no wish to intrude on your private affairs, Miss Smith,' Dilys said, choosing her words firmly, 'but for your own sake she feels she should point out that you are not acting wisely.'

'Wisely?' Augusta Smith's unoccupied face showed signs of life. It went through the preliminaries for laughter, her mouth stretched, her cheeks dimpled, and then she put back her head and howled.

As an expression of misery it was more than adequate. She wept with appetite for sorrow and an ingestion of it as greedy as a child's. The room hooted and re-hooted with her boohoos, people froze in surprise.

Gwen and Dilys froze too, Dilys only momentarily. She leaned across and held the knuckles which Augusta was grinding into her eye-sockets.

'Stop it!' She pulled Augusta's hands and slapped them. Augusta bayed her unhappiness to the ceiling. 'Help me get her out!'

Between them Gwen and Dilys walked her from the dining-room. She made no objection, she went, lamenting in a public way as if for the sorrow of mankind.

Dilys left Gwen to take her upstairs. She saw no reason for disrupting their meal.

'Put her in her room and come down and finish your dinner,' she told Gwen, and was irritated to see faces turn to her when she went back to the dining-room.

'A slight case of over-excitement,' she said with a smile and lift of her shoulders.

'There's something wrong with that girl,' declared Mrs. Punsett.

'Nonsense, she's an American.'

Dilys left them to decide whether that was in Augusta's favour or otherwise. The risotto was congealing on their plates and it would be a pity to drink the Chablis now.

Gwen came back looking troubled. 'Dilly, I'm so sorry—'

'It wasn't your fault.'

'I feel it may help her to let go. I know we can't take on any of her unhappiness for her but if we can spread it a little—'

'The brandy made her maudlin. She has an unstable personality.'

'Dilly, I can't just ignore her—'

'You feel responsible for her?'

'Yes.' Gwen picked up the Chablis. 'Someone should be.'

'I thought we'd cork that and have it tomorrow.'

'Oh damn, let's have it now. I need it.'

But the wine didn't help. As Dilys had expected it succumbed to the greasy rice. They finished it with the Diplomat, which was also a mistake. Gwen, becoming slightly fretful about food, said that she ought to diet.

'I've put on half a stone. I wonder if I'm eating to compensate for losing Arnold?'

'What was Miss Smith doing when you left her?'

'I gave her some sleeping tablets to take. They're quite harmless and non-habit-forming. My doctor prescribed them after Arnold — As a matter of fact I've taken hardly any. I still have enough left to dope an army.'

They had always been able to communicate their thoughts — whole sequences sometimes. So it was quite likely now that although nothing was actually spoken there would be recriminations and perhaps a despairing attempt at an excuse and a long-long-lasting apology without one word ever passing between them.

As they sat looking at each other several things happened, the same several things to them both — awful, ineluctable, irrevocable things, and in the twinkling of an eye. They rose from the table as one.

Augusta Smith was on her knees beside the bed. Her nose was pressed into the down quilt, causing her to breathe sideways like a showy swimmer doing the crawl. It took a great deal of effort getting each snoring breath and she probably couldn't have kept it up much longer. She clutched an empty chemist's bottle and a toothbrush.

Gwen screamed.

'Get salt and a tablespoon,' said Dilys.

'She's killed herself!'

Dilys pushed Gwen bodily out of the door. 'Plenty of salt and don't tell anyone what it's for.'

Augusta was surprisingly heavy, an all-American girl fed on milk and steak. Dilys pulled her away from the bed and forced open her jaws. One small white pill still stuck to her underlip, her tongue was coated and malodorous which was not surprising the way she had been treating herself. When Dilys tried to get her on to her feet she rallied and resisted. Dilys struggled and was suddenly draped with her as she lost consciousness. They fell together across the bed.

Finally Dilys managed to get her face down, with her head hanging over the side. She gripped her chin and pressed her thumb on the back of the girl's tongue. . . .

Gwen came back with the salt.

'Two tablespoonfuls in a glass of warm water. Hurry!'

They pulled Augusta into a sitting position. There was something nursery-like about her then, legs stuck out straight, toes up, her long hair shocked over her face.

'Support her shoulders,' said Dilys, 'while I get some of this down.'

It was like trying to fill a buttonhole which kept changing shape. 'It's a good sign,' said Dilys. 'She's not lapsing into a coma.'

'She isn't swallowing! She's holding it in her mouth!'

Dilys grasped Augusta's cheeks between her fingertips as she would a small balloon. The salt water jetted out of Augusta's mouth.

'She needs a stomach pump. We'll have to get a doctor.'

'Dilly, she's going to die!'

'Ring through to the desk and tell Doris to get Dr. Schwartz here quick. Then come and help me keep her alive. Hurry!'

Augusta showed signs of sinking, literally. She fell forward into her own lap and from there to the floor where she lay curled up, faintly smiling as if she had never been born and was still in the safety of the womb.

'It's an emergency!' Gwen was crying into the telephone. 'We want the doctor immediately — yes — there's been an accident —'

'Tell her to tell him it's barbiturate poisoning.'

'Oh my God, it's all my fault —'

'Damn you, yes!' Dilys knelt on the floor and slapped at Augusta's cheeks. They each had distinct impressions that it was Gwen's face being slapped — Gwen felt the shock and Dilys a grim satisfaction. But Gwen also sensed Dilys's satisfaction and Dilys Gwen's shock. Something which had always been at half latch in their relationship clicked finally home.

The doctor took fifteen minutes to come, the longest fifteen minutes they had spent together. They hauled Augusta Smith up and down the length of the room. She hung on them like a sack of shifting sand, at one moment top-heavy, the next her whole weight dropped to her thighs. Her legs buckled and she slid out of their arms a dozen times.

Gwen was soon panting and crimson with effort. Dilys was merciless, she pumped Augusta's arms and kicked her feet one before the other in the motion of walking. Once Gwen stumbled and they scrambled together on the floor as if in some awful romp.

'Dilly, I can't get my breath—'

'If you wait to get yours she'll lose hers.' Dilys seized Augusta and shook her. The girl's head rolled with a sickening sound from the gristle in the bones of her neck.

'Oh God!' moaned Gwen.

Dilys rounded on her. 'I'm picking up after you!'

Dr. Schwartz found them staggering to and fro, Augusta's head between their shoulders and her last consciousness gone down into her feet which were paddling slightly in a reflex protest. He took in the situation at a glance.

'Get her on the bed.' He was a man of few words, which Gwen found alarming.

'She's been sick,' said Dilys, 'but not enough.'

'Let me see.' He pointed to the bowl and Gwen turned away. But he pinned her with, 'Barbiturates? What barbiturates has she had?'

'I don't know, they were to help me to sleep. My doctor gave them to me—'

'As I assumed,' said Dr. Schwartz, 'since I have not prescribed a thing of the sort for Miss Craig or for anyone here recently. What was in them?'

'They were just little white tablets—'

'Another bowl, please, and a towel.' He snapped open his bag. 'Miss Craig, what has been happening?'

'This girl stole a bottle of sleeping pills from my friend, Mrs. Beaumont, and swallowed them all.'

'Stole?'

'The bottle certainly wasn't given to her,' said Dilys and held the doctor's stare until he turned back to his patient. 'Do you wish us to stay?'

'This one—' he lifted Augusta's eyelid—'she is not a friend?'

'She's a hotel guest, that's entirely all she is,' said Dilys.

'Unless you wish to see me use a stomach-pump you need not stay. I will speak with you afterwards.'

'I'll be in my office.'

They encountered Mrs. Punsett on the stairs. She had been hoping that while the doctor was here—yes, she had recognised his bag which was certainly not an overnight bag—he would take a look at her heart. It was so seldom that she had a chance of medical attention, the General was set against it and she could never actually call in a doctor. Would Mrs. Beaumont, dear kind Mrs. Beaumont, allow the examination to take place in Mrs. Beaumont's room so that the General need not know—

'I'm afraid not,' Dilys told her. 'Dr. Schwartz is here to see Miss Smith and when he has seen her he will want to see Mrs. Beaumont and me.'

'Oh, are you all ill?'

'No, dear,' said Gwen, 'only Augusta. It's another thing with us.'

Being Gwen she overdid the secrecy. She closed the door of Dilys's office and turning her back against it asked in a whisper if Augusta would live.

'She *could*—' Dilys began deliberately loud and clear, and then relented, for this was Gwen's way of helping herself through what she had been and what she had done. She was like one who can face disaster only by attending furiously to details. 'I think she will,' Dilys said kindly. 'I hope she will.'

'I did mean to bring that bottle of pills away with me, Dilly—'

'I know. Do you remember the bean bag?'

'What?'

'The day we first met, at school.'

'Why do you remember that?' Gwen sounded fretful. She was remembering, at that moment, how Dilys had damned her. After forty-five years of friendship Dilys had turned round—people always said that, but this time it was true and Dilys had turned and said, 'Damn you!'—for a lapse of memory, because Gwen had not actually carried out something which she had fully wished and intended to do. Surely the wish should count towards the deed? Surely good faith should carry a little weight? Gwen's nose pricked with tears.

'Of course—' Dilys was following her own line of thought which was certainly not Gwen's—'she'll need nursing for a day or two and we can't cope with that here. She'll have to go.'

'Go?'

'To hospital or somewhere. She may try again.'

'Oh Dilly, do you think she will?'

'It's possible.' Dilys went to the mirror to tidy up. She touched herself so deftly and impersonally it was always a fascination to Gwen to watch. 'I want her off the premises before she does.'

'But she mustn't be allowed to try again!'

'Therefore she must be in a place where they will restrain her.'

Gwen shivered and Dilys added sharply, 'She has a psychopathic sickness.'

Was that what it was? Was that the actual technical thing?

'She was so miserable. Oh Dilly, you know how ridiculously happy and unhappy you can be when you're young—'

'We're not qualified to treat that kind of thing.'

Yes, it was possible to do harm while wishing to do good and it was possible and very probable that not being able to stand the sight of unhappiness was a wholly selfish reaction.

'We've just seen how it turns out when we try.'

Dilys put her arm about Gwen's shoulders and Gwen cried for a number of reasons—gratitude mostly.

The Proper Study
of *Woman is Man*

THERE was a suggestion in the way they got into the train that their worlds differed and they were cohabiting, uneasily, this mutual one on the Brighton line. He peeled off his coat and opened his shoulders as if the carriage was a bubble which he wanted to burst. She moved providently in the limited space and sat down with care. She was taking her place among her kind and as she positioned her bag, gloves and newspaper on her lap she smiled a general smile. That these people were not his kind was apparent by his dropping himself wholesale into a seat. He spread wide his knees and sighed down his nose.

Someone said to her, 'You weren't on the six-eight last night.'

'I stayed up to see the Leonardo drawings.'

'Good?'

'Wonderful.' She laughed. 'I kept thinking, I can't even draw a line.'

As the train pulled out of Burgess Hill he relapsed into an uncompliant heap with the intention, the determination it seemed, of staying heaped throughout the journey. Someone in the corridor waved to her. Smiling her general smile she unfolded her *Telegraph*.

The chipper bungalows flashed past, dewy-roofed, windows bloomed. The train settled to the track and the passengers were gently mobile in their clothes and rubbed along to the one rhythm. She found him gazing at her with half-closed eyes as if he were calculating the dimensions of her face. Or he was sleepy.

She was irritated by the way he sprawled in his seat, knees straining at the crease in his trousers. She took a biro from her bag and turned to the crossword. In the margin of the page she wrote 'Oaf!'

'I didn't have my ticket punched.' He leaned towards her and she added ears and legs and made 'Oaf!' into a dog.

'Why don't you get a season?'

'I may not stay a season.'

'Oh I think you'll like living down here. There are so many compensations.'

'For what?'

'The travelling—two and a half hours every day. But of course you like travelling.'

Crying 'Huh!' he flung himself back in his seat and gazed up at the luggage rack.

Her cheeks pinkened but she said calmly, 'You'll get used to it. I hardly notice the journey, in fact it's rather a welcome breathing space at each end of the day. I shouldn't care to live in London or the suburbs. Especially at this time of year.'

The gardens were stuffed with daffodils, King Alfreds by the ton. Passed at speed they battered the eye and the train's noise was yellow.

'Egg and spinach.' Eyes half shut, he watched through the window. Did he prefer not to see things clearly or was it just a habit he had got into with squinting against the sun? 'What do you do when you get back there? Tonight, what are you doing tonight?'

'It's my brother's birthday. We're taking him to dinner and a show at the Dome.'

'And tomorrow?'

'I shall probably stay at home and do some sewing.'

'And the week-end? I'm worried about week-ends. You see,

I've just had Friday to Monday at Owlswick and you may not believe this, but I've never been aware of the week-end till now. It's a British invention.'

'Well, but you've lived in Christian countries, surely?'

'When I was a boy the week-end didn't exist. My parents had a pub, one opening time was the same as another.'

'We look forward to the week-end. Heavens, I don't know what we'd do without it. It's a sort of a junction — you'll feel the same.'

She returned to her crossword. The 'Oaf!' dog now gave her an idea for a two-headed monster, drawing which she became completely absorbed.

'If I want to feel the same.'

She raised her eyebrows and he too seemed to realise that it was rather rude because he said impatiently, 'Oh well, I've obviously got to settle down as they say.'

'Do they?'

'If I've heard that phrase once I've heard it fifty times.'

'Why did you come back?'

'Health.'

She had noted, with approval, how evident his bones were. She liked men to be rugged.

'Another year in the tropics would finish me, according to the doctors.' He said gloomily, 'As if an English winter could set anyone up.'

'There's the summer to look forward to. We have beautiful summers here and when it rains that's beautiful too. Unless you're fearfully adventurous there's no lack of things to do.'

'Like what?'

'Swimming, sailing, tennis —'

'I can't hold a racket and I shouldn't be much use in a boat.' He showed her the palm of his right hand and she drew in her breath sharply and compassionately.

'What happened? Were you bitten?'

'Some bite.'

'By a lion or a tiger, I meant.'

'You may not believe this, but I didn't see such a beast the whole time I was in Africa. They're mostly in the game reserves. People think it's all tom-toms and Tarzan of the Apes. Well, it's not. It's—'

The train ran into a cutting and she could not hear. She saw that he was smiling, probably at what he was leaving unsaid.

'—one remove from brutes,' was audible as the train ran out of the cutting.

'If you were telling me how you got your scar I didn't hear a word.'

'I wasn't. I was talking about Africa. The other's a bit grisly.'

She raised her brows again. In fact she wanted to hear the story but to him she looked sceptical, and before she had heard a word of it. She had made up her mind to disbelieve. When had she done that? With what right or reason?

'It isn't fit to tell you.'

This time she lifted her chin, quite sharply, and the gesture—or indeed anything she could have done, or not done, at that point—was enough to start him talking.

'I got this from some people who were on the run from civilisation. Every time it got near them they moved deeper into the jungle. Church, Government, social services, even science had had a go at them. That's why I was there, to collect facts for a survey of tribal systems.

'They called themselves the Sky People and their chief—I called him "Sky High"—swore he was born of a cloud. That was the only nice thing about them. Dirty, cruel beggars they were.'

'Cruel?'

'Funny, wasn't it, they were ready to die to keep the tribe pure and almost any other mixture would have improved them.'

The carriage filled at Haywards Heath, bodies passed between them and knees hemmed them in. When he could see her again he went on.

'They did everything the way they always had, it was death to change a ritual. If a cooking-pot wore out they had to get a special rigmajig pronounced by the chief before they could use a new one. It was no surprise to me that they were still making living sacrifices.'

The man next to him was listening and it vexed her, quite unreasonably vexed her with him, that this man should openly eavesdrop. The story, grisly or no, was being told for her benefit.

But the eavesdropper had not seen the scar and she was glad that it was a secret between them, curled in the palm of his damaged hand.

'I had a fellow, Dave Cathcart, with me, straight from college and full of flowerpower. He wanted to civilise them. "They need a school, and medicine, and pinafores", he kept telling me. I said to let them alone, we were only there to observe.'

'Pinafores?'

'The women were just big monkeys.' He stared round the carriage as if expecting an argument, then leaned forward and whispered loudly. 'I knew old Sky High was up to something. They'd been getting ready for days and when we arrived it was already in hand and they couldn't back down for fear of upsetting the sky spirits. Cathcart found them in the middle of a ceremony of purification and threw up on the spot. He had a weak stomach. I told him they were going to offer up a living sacrifice—he wasn't happy with the idea of butchering a goat on the altar.'

'Were you?'

'I knew it was going to be a human sacrifice.'

Their knees touched and she moved hers, not wishing—not at this juncture—to make physical contact. Not that he was distasteful to her, she simply knew that this was the wrong moment.

The eavesdropper leaned closer—him she found repugnant.

'Cathcart would have tried to stop it if he'd known.'

'Didn't you try?'

'What would have been the use? I couldn't make them better ju-ju.'

'But it was—' She was about to say 'barbarous', then it struck her that she might as well say that grass was green—'it was murder. You had something—a conscience, principle, didn't you?'

'It was ritual murder,' he amended, 'that was *their* principle. I didn't have any as far as they were concerned, I'd stopped thinking I knew what was good and what was bad out there. You'd have to be born again to know that.'

'What about the victim? Didn't you think of him?'

'Yes, a lot. It was a girl, girls were the supreme offering. The Sky People reckoned they offered up the generations unborn when they sacrificed a girl.'

She had been told that she was a good listener. She considered it a useful attribute, and valuable on occasion. As a rule, she did not think about listening, merely did it and with no trouble voided her mind for the reception of someone else's. Now she felt some tiny intrusions of her own, they could hardly be called thought, they were more like the pricklings of consciousness.

'Surely *someone* showed some responsibility?'

She saw that she had used the wrong word. Obviously it had unpleasant associations, seemed to him to be directly to blame. He spat it out.

'Responsibility!' and sat back in his seat and said with angry indifference, 'Cathcart did. He found them actually at it and stopped the show. Next day he was dead.'

She said patiently but firmly, 'What happened?'

'They killed him. There wasn't a mark on him, except his

own pimples, he was a pimply youth. They just fixed for his heart to stop. Know how it's done? Neatest trick in the world.'

He smiled without rancour at his damaged hand. 'Sky High did this to me. He was for killing Cathcart on the spot. Dave had destroyed the ju-ju, you see, and insulted the gods. Sky High went after him with the sacrificial knife. I got between them and got the knife through my hand.'

'How awful.' She said, 'I knew you would have done something,' and looked calmly at him.

'Well, that's all I did and it was too much for me and not enough for Dave. He was dead anyway next day and I had to take him to Nairobi. Six days with a corpse and a festering hand in a filthy little paddle-boat on the Zambesi.'

'Excuse me,' said the eavesdropper, 'the Zambesi rises in Angola.'

'What?'

'Its mouth is in Mozambique.'

'What are you talking about?'

'The Zambesi's nowhere near Nairobi.'

'Who said it was?'

She stood up. 'Come into the corridor where we can be private.'

'What a fool!' he said loudly but he got up and followed her out of the carriage. She was relieved, after all she didn't know what to expect from him.

'That fool!' To her surprise he was smiling. 'Did you ever hear anything like it?'

'It was an unwarranted intrusion.'

'Excuse him, he said! He's a pedant, I can't stand pedantry.' He looked at her soberly. 'I do know about Africa, you know.'

'Of course.'

They leaned on the window bar watching woods slip by. The spring leaves lay back like ears with the passing of the train.

She sighed. 'I'm always sorry when we lose sight of the Downs. I love them—now I do. I hardly noticed them once.' But she believed that there was a time for everything and that without the conjunction of time, or with the wrong conjunction, events misfired or did not happen at all.

'I was coming back from Ringmer one night when the car broke down. It was about two a.m., in a fold of the Downs, right at the very bottom, so I couldn't even coast. No one came. I sat listening to the foxes. You know they make an awful noise, a scream followed by a sort of whistling breath, but I didn't mind. I liked it, I didn't want to come away. All things being equal I'd still be there. Of course I finally had to get out and fix the car, but ever since I've had a special feeling about the Downs.'

'*You* fixed it?'

'It was only a blocked jet.'

'My truck broke down in the desert once and I was walking for three days. At least it didn't so much break down, it was sabotaged. Damned Arabs probably filled the spare jerry-cans with water instead of petrol.'

'People haven't been very kind to you, have they?'

He looked surprised. 'Oh, I don't know. I certainly hope they will be.'

'Are you worried about starting this new job?'

'I'm certainly apprehensive.'

'You needn't be. With your experience of the desert and the jungle you'll be able to cope with company directors.'

'You're laughing at me!'

'No.'

He put his head down on his arms. 'I don't know how I'll be, taped to a desk. I've never stayed anywhere more than a few weeks.'

'Too much change is as bad as too little.' Actually she thought it worse, it seemed to her a terribly damaging admission. 'You'll get over it.' She decided that Fate had made him suffer, though not needlessly, for obviously there was something to be made good, to be made up.

'I came back to stay alive, it'll be ironic if all I do is congeal. Like that fool in there. What does he know about Africa?'

'I think he must be excused. After all, he's stayed and worked at living and I think, whether we like it or not, we all have to do that. And it's harder here than where you've been—'

'Harder to jellify!'

His voice was muffled and it occurred to her that he was crying.

She said briskly, 'You can't be disinvolved, you know, like you were out there. You'd have to be born again you said, to have principles, and I think you were right. I think you'd have to be born right outside Europe.'

'I'm not cold-blooded!'

'There's so much more competition here—' her voice softened—'for what you want.'

He raised his blotched face and asked, 'What do I want?'

She knew better than to answer. She said, 'I usually go along to the buffet car for a coffee after Three Bridges.'